Thou Art With Me

Other Books by Debbie Viguié

The Psalm 23 Mysteries

The Lord is My Shepherd
I Shall Not Want
Lie Down in Green Pastures
Beside Still Waters
Restoreth My Soul
In the Paths of Righteousness
For His Name's Sake
Walk Through the Valley
The Shadow of Death
I Will Fear No Evil

The Kiss Trilogy

Kiss of Night
Kiss of Death
Kiss of Revenge

Sweet Seasons

The Summer of Cotton Candy
The Fall of Candy Corn
The Winter of Candy Canes
The Spring of Candy Apples

Witch Hunt

The Thirteenth Sacrifice
The Last Grave
Circle of Blood

Tex Ravencroft Adventures (with Dr. Scott Viguié)

The Tears of Poseidon

Thou Art With Me

Psalm 23 Mysteries

By Debbie Viguié

Published by Big Pink Bow

Thou Art With Me

Copyright © 2015 by Debbie Viguié

ISBN-13: 978-0-9906971-3-8

Published by Big Pink Bow

www.bigpinkbow.com

All rights reserved.

Dedicated to Becky Lewis, a true fan of the series and a wonderful supporter.

Thank you to everyone who helped make this book a reality, particularly Scott Viguié, Barbara Reynolds, Rick Reynolds and Calliope Collacott. Thank you to all the fans of the series for your support, encouragement, and enthusiasm. Thank you to Susan George, a dedicated fan, who correctly guessed exactly who would be taking Cindy dress shopping in this book. Great job, Susan!

1

Detective Mark Walters had always had great respect for Wednesdays. He wasn't sure why, but Wednesdays, though they were in the middle of the week, had always signified endings and beginnings for him. This Wednesday he wasn't sure which one it was going to be. He just knew that his captain had ordered him into his office nearly twenty minutes earlier and had yet to join him.

Mentally he was going over everything he could have possibly done over the last few weeks that might have gotten him into trouble. He was drawing a complete blank. Things had been fairly quiet since just before Christmas. Now it was February and he had really been enjoying the respite. Liam and he had even managed to close two cold cases in that time.

The door opened and his captain stormed in. His face was like a thundercloud and he glared at Mark as he took his seat behind his desk. The captain didn't like him, he'd never made any bones about that. Mark couldn't blame him. In the last two years in particular he hadn't exactly been the model detective.

His captain glared at him and Mark waited, knowing that sooner or later the man would have to tell him what this was all about.

"You're a pain in the butt. You know that, right?" the captain finally asked.

Mark cleared his throat. "You're not the first to suggest that."

"I should have gotten rid of you over that whole Green Pastures incident."

Mark took a steadying breath before saying, "But you didn't."

"You color outside the lines. You involve civilians in criminal investigations. Worst of all, you never know when to let something go."

Mark was beginning to wonder if his ongoing investigations surrounding the mystery of his late partner, Paul, were at the heart of whatever it was that was eating the captain. He managed to keep his mouth shut, though. It was better to be told what was wrong than to start making guesses and risk really getting on the other man's bad side.

"A friend of mine from college went missing from one of those tree-hugging wellness centers last week and I can't get any straight answers about what might have happened to him."

Mark had no idea what that had to do with him, but he just nodded, waiting for the captain to continue and hopefully shed some light on everything.

"Either no one knows what happened to him or no one's talking. His wife is beside herself and she's been after me to try and find out what happened."

The man paused long enough to give Mark another good, long glare. Mark couldn't stand it anymore, he had to at least say something. "Can't you speak with the local police?"

"I've tried, but no one wants to touch this thing with a ten foot pole."

"Why not?" Mark heard himself asking.

"Because this center is on an Indian reservation a couple of miles from one of the biggest casinos in this state."

Mark shook his head. "The local police should be able to investigate."

"They should be able to, but they seem very uninterested in doing so."

"That sounds like a real problem," Mark said, still wondering what this had to do with him.

"It is, and it needs solving. You know what the good news is? The center is hosting a couples' retreat next week."

"How is that good news?"

"I can put someone in there undercover and get to the bottom of this whole mess."

Suddenly things made a lot more sense. "To a couples' retreat? Look, sir, if I get the direction you're drifting there's no way I could ask Traci to do something like that, especially not with the twins to take care of."

The captain narrowed his eyes. "I'm well aware of your family's needs," he said. "Besides, I can't risk sending in a cop, violating federal laws and the sovereignty of the tribe."

"Then what are you talking about?" Mark asked.

"I'm talking about your penchant for not doing things by the book. I want you to get your friends to do it."

Mark frowned. "I don't think Geanie and Joseph would be up for tackling something like that."

"I'm not talking about them. I'm talking about the other ones, the church secretary and the rabbi."

Mark was stunned. "You want me to send Cindy and Jeremiah in undercover to a potentially dangerous place where we have no jurisdiction?"

"That's exactly what I want you to do."

"You're crazy." The words slipped out before Mark could stop them. He cringed inwardly, but didn't bother trying to take them back.

"I was crazy for keeping you on here after what happened. Now it's time you did something for me."

Mark didn't like this and he didn't want any part of it. Looking at the other man, though, he saw the desperation in his eyes, and that was something Mark understood all too well. The captain was right. He had played fast and loose with the rules before and this was what he had coming to him for it.

"They're not going to like this," he said.

"Make them like it," the captain said. "I'll provide what support I can, but given the circumstances..."

"It won't be much," Mark filled in. "Anything else?"

"Yeah, remember that this is strictly off the books."

"I understand. I'll go talk to Cindy and Jeremiah."

Jeremiah was in the synagogue office having one of the more unpleasant conversations he'd had with his secretary, Marie, in a long time.

"You shouldn't be with that Gentile woman," Marie said.

Jeremiah had pointed out to her on multiple occasions that he was pretty sure she was the only one who used that word anymore, but it never did any good. Of course, defending his friendship with Cindy never worked either, but he knew he was going to try again to do so.

"Cindy and I aren't together," Jeremiah said wearily.

"Then you're lying either to yourself or to me," Marie said stubbornly.

Jeremiah had no desire to discuss his love life with anyone, least of all Marie. "What do you want from me?"

"I want you to trust that God will bring the woman he wants you to marry into your life. I want you to keep an open mind and ask for a sign."

"I do trust God in this matter and I do want to follow where He leads."

"Really?" she demanded, crossing her arms over her chest. "You'll be open?"

"Yes."

"Then humor me, the next single woman who walks through that door I want you to give serious consideration to marrying."

Before Jeremiah could say anything the door opened. Marie turned, a look of triumphant expectation on her face.

Cindy walked in and Jeremiah's heart skipped a beat. Marie's expression turned to one of dismay.

"You know, Marie, you were so right," Jeremiah said, walking toward Cindy.

"Am I interrupting?" Cindy asked, looking hesitantly first at him then at Marie.

"No, your timing couldn't have been more perfect. Marie just told me that I should give serious consideration to marrying you," Jeremiah said.

"She did?" Cindy asked, clearly startled.

He glanced at Marie and couldn't keep himself from smirking. He toyed with the idea of kissing Cindy in front of her just to get her goat. He decided against it, though. The relationship with Cindy was not something he was willing to share with the outside world. Not just yet.

"What's up?" he asked.

"Can I talk to you for a minute?" Cindy asked.

"Sure, come into my office," Jeremiah said.

Cindy walked inside and Jeremiah closed the door behind them. He had an almost uncontrollable urge to kiss her then, but he restrained himself.

"So, what did you want to talk about?" he said, standing as close to her as he could get without actually touching her.

"A week from Saturday the church has decided to host a big dinner."

"Okay," he said, not sure what that would have to do with him.

"Some of my coworkers have asked me to work that evening and help things go smoothly."

"And you don't want to work at the event? How come?" he asked.

She was staring at him like he was an idiot. A few seconds passed and then she said, "Are you seriously asking me why I don't want to work at an event next Saturday?"

"Yes," he said, still not following.

"Valentine's Day?"

"Oh," he said, suddenly realizing what was going on. "Oh, Valentine's Day. I'm sorry, I didn't realize...I mean, I've never had any cause to celebrate the day before."

She just stared at him, clearly waiting for him to continue.

He took a deep breath. "Of course you can't work that night. You'll just have to tell your bosses you have a date."

"I do?" she said, starting to smile.

"Yes."

"Can I tell them with who?" she asked.

He was a bit taken aback. He was by nature and by necessity intensely private. Of course, it seemed like everyone was already making assumptions about them.

"It's okay, I won't tell them with who," she said before he could respond. She stood on tiptoe and kissed him on the cheek.

She stepped back just as his office door opened. Startled, he looked over, wondering why Marie hadn't warned him he was about to have a visitor.

Mark walked through the door, his face grim, and shut it behind himself. "Oh good, you're both here," the detective said.

"And I'm guessing since you're here in person and not just calling on the phone that something bad has happened," Jeremiah said.

"Yes, no, maybe, that's the heck of it."

"Okay, what's going on?" Cindy asked, exchanging a quick glance with Jeremiah.

"My captain has ordered me to ask you two for your help."

There was definitely something off in the other man's behavior, and Jeremiah was certain that whatever Mark was about to say he really wished he didn't have to.

"What kind of help?"

Mark sat down on the couch with a weary sigh. "An old friend of his went missing while at a wellness center spa retreat sort of thing. He can't get any straight answers and he's naturally worried."

"And that sounds like a job for the local police," Cindy said.

"It should be, but they're not cooperating. To complicate things, the center is on tribal land so we can't send any of our people in there to investigate without risking a total and complete disaster."

"So, you want us to go," Jeremiah guessed.

"And the Samaritan wins the prize," Mark said.

Mark hadn't called him that in a long time and Jeremiah felt himself tensing. Mark wasn't happy about the situation which meant that there was likely an elevated risk of danger. "Not a Samaritan, Jewish," he replied perfunctorily.

"Frankly what you'll be is a saint if you agree to go through with this," Mark muttered.

"Why don't you just tell us exactly what it is we're supposed to do?" Cindy asked.

"My boss wants the two of you to go in undercover at the wellness center as just a couple of customers and sniff around and see what you can find out."

"When?" Jeremiah asked.

"Starting Monday."

"Why wait so long?" Cindy asked.

"Because that's when the center's week-long couples' retreat starts. You can go in, pose as a married couple, and hopefully find out what there is to find out fast."

Cindy blushed. "No," she said.

"No, you won't do it?" Mark asked.

"I can go in undercover if you really need me to, but we're not going to pose as a married couple."

"It's not like you guys haven't done that before," Mark said, sounding puzzled.

Jeremiah struggled to keep his expression neutral. Back in Israel Cindy had told him that she wanted to stop pretending that she was his wife when they ended up in difficult circumstances. He understood why she was objecting to what Mark was suggesting even if the detective did not.

"Can non-married couples participate in the retreat?" Jeremiah asked.

"I would think so, but I'll double check," Mark said.

"If they can, then we'll help," Cindy told him.

"Give me a minute to find out," Mark said as he pulled his phone out of his pocket.

While Mark made his phone call Cindy gazed intently at the ground, not wanting to meet Jeremiah's eyes. She had meant what she'd said back in July. It was too hard masquerading as his wife and she didn't want to have to do that again. She knew Mark didn't understand, but there was no way she was going to explain herself to him.

A couple minutes passed before Mark ended his call. "You're in. As a dating couple. Good?"

She nodded. Not trusting herself to speak.

"I swear, first the captain then you guys, everyone's getting weird on me," Mark muttered.

Now that it was settled another problem occurred to her. "I really don't have any more sick time or vacation time coming to me for a while."

Mark scowled. "I'll talk to your business manager. Hopefully we can work something out."

"Okay."

"Let's get that taken care of now," Mark said. "Unless the two of you aren't finished discussing whatever you were discussing when I came in."

"No, we were finished," Jeremiah said quickly.

"Good. The sooner we get this all taken care of the sooner the captain will get off my back."

Cindy and Mark left together. She stole a quick glance at Marie who was still scowling at her. She hadn't had a chance to ask Jeremiah what he had been discussing with his secretary when Cindy came in the office. She'd have to remember to do that. Whatever it was, she was positive that Marie had not been urging Jeremiah to marry her.

"That woman glares an awful lot," Mark noted after they had left the office.

"She doesn't like me."

"I'm not sure she likes anybody."

They walked the rest of the way in silence. They finally reached the church office and Mark walked into Sylvia's office to talk to her while Cindy made a beeline for Geanie, her friend and the church's graphic designer.

"What is it? You've got a weird look on your face," Geanie said as she looked up from a bulletin she was proofreading.

"Mark's asked me to go undercover at a couples' retreat with Jeremiah."

"That should be...interesting," Geanie said with a smirk.

"I shouldn't do it," Cindy said. "I've got so much work to do in the next week."

"Consider it officially covered. You know I get bored if I don't have enough to do anyway and this is a slow time of the year for me."

"Thanks."

Cindy had known that Geanie would be willing to help out. That wasn't really what was bothering her. It was going to be strange, pretending a level of intimacy with Jeremiah that they didn't have even though they were in a quasi-relationship, if it could even really be called that.

She took a deep breath. She was worrying when she shouldn't be. They'd probably be so busy trying to find out what had happened to the missing man that they wouldn't have time to think about their relationship, let alone discuss it.

Although it might be a good thing if they did. If someone had actually asked her to describe their relationship she wasn't sure that she could. At least they were actually going to go out on Valentine's Day. That was something she could hold onto.

It would actually be her first Valentine's Day that she had someone, and from what Jeremiah had said it sounded like it would be his first as well.

"You're glowing," Geanie said, interrupting her train of thought.

"Excuse me?"

"You glow when you think about Jeremiah. You have for a while but lately it's been so much stronger, you just get this radiant sort of smile."

Cindy felt herself blushing. "I just hope everything works out at this retreat," she mumbled.

"A week together at a couples' retreat bonding, solving a mystery, what could possibly go wrong?" Geanie asked with a grin.

2

Mark was worried. So many things could go wrong with Cindy and Jeremiah going undercover at the couples' retreat. He'd stopped counting when he'd reached seventeen possibilities, each of them worse than the last. Half a dozen times he'd decided to march into his captain's office and tell the man that this was folly and it wasn't going to happen.

And half a dozen times he'd sat back down. Given how much slack the captain cut him, and all he and the department had done off the books for Cindy and Jeremiah, the three of them kind of owed him.

Cars weren't allowed at the retreat center, one of their weird quirks. Apparently taking away someone's means of escape forced them to stay and work things out with their significant other. It was just one more thing that made him nervous about the entire situation. It was also one more thing pointing to foul play being at the heart of whatever had happened to the captain's friend.

So, Mark had volunteered to drop them off there on Sunday. At least that way he could get a quick lay of the land, know where he had to go if he needed to ride to the rescue, so to speak.

Liam was in court testifying on an older case that had finally come to trial. That left Mark in the office pushing papers around his desk and going slowly out of his mind. It wasn't pretty. He was staring at one particular file and he realized he'd read the same paragraph three times when he heard a woman address him.

Mark looked up and started, his entire body jerking in shock.

Georgia Dryer was standing there. Tall, slender, and just as aristocratic looking as the last time he'd seen her. She was wearing a tailored charcoal gray suit with a splash of red at her waist.

Georgia had been Paul's estranged wife, widow now. She had been living on the other side of the country for at least ten months before Paul was killed. She hadn't come out for the funeral and Mark hadn't had any communication with her since. He'd left a couple of messages for her, none of which she'd returned. He hadn't been in any shape to really talk to her anyway right after it happened.

He rose to his feet unsteadily. "Georgia, what can I do for you?"

"Hello, Mark. It's been a long time."

He didn't know what to say. He would have been shocked if she had called him out of the blue, but here she was standing in front of him thousands of miles away from where she should be.

"Yes," he said, still at a loss for words.

He glanced around. None of the other officers were paying attention. Why would they? He'd only ever seen Georgia a handful of times and Paul had been his partner for years. None of the others had likely ever laid eyes on her.

He forced himself to take a deep breath. "Maybe we should go somewhere that we can talk."

She nodded.

13

Mark grabbed his coat off the back of his chair and led the way outside.

"Did you drive?" he asked.

"I took a taxi."

"Okay."

He got into his car and after a momentary hesitation she got into the passenger's seat.

Paul's seat.

No, he told himself sternly. If it was anyone's seat, it was Liam's now. Paul had been gone for nearly two years. It was strange how in a moment all the pain and confusion of losing his partner and discovering that the man wasn't who he thought he was could all come roaring back.

"Shall we get some coffee?" he asked, hearing the strain in his voice as his throat clenched.

"I'd prefer not to be seen," she murmured.

He resisted the urge to point out that she'd shown up at his office. She had probably known he was the only one there who would recognize her. With the rest of the town, though, that might not be the case.

They couldn't go to his house. Traci and the babies were there and it would be chaos. Plus he wanted to hear for himself what Georgia had to say before dragging anyone else into it.

He pulled his phone out of his pocket and fired off a text to Joseph. *U at home?*

No, came back the reply almost instantly.

Need to borrow your house for a couple of hours.

U know the alarm code.

It was true. Mark did know the alarm code. And at some point during their many misadventures he had even acquired a key which he had kept.

"I know somewhere we can go," he said, putting his phone away and starting up the car.

As they drove he couldn't think of a thing to say and she seemed to be content to let the silence stretch on between them. When they finally turned up the drive toward Joseph and Geanie's mansion she turned and looked at him with sudden curiosity.

"You know the Coulters?"

"Been friends a couple of years now. Traci was one of the bridesmaids in their wedding," he said.

He certainly had her attention now.

"What is Joseph's wife like? When I heard about the wedding I couldn't imagine what type of woman had finally ensnared him."

"Trust me, the ensnaring was mutual. How did you hear about the wedding?"

"When one of the wealthiest bachelors in the country gets married, it's news," she said.

Georgia had always been interested in high society. The irony was that Joseph most certainly was not. Mark had long suspected that she had married Paul because of the family name that came attached and the prospect of inheriting quite a lot when his parents died. It turned out she didn't like being a cop's wife, though, and over the years the fights had escalated until she moved to New York where she became the editor at a fashion magazine. She had kept the last name, though, along with the ring which Mark noticed she was still wearing.

As they pulled up in front of the house he saw her eyes grow enormous as she took in the mansion. "What a magnificent place to entertain," she said at last.

"Yeah. Their Halloween party was killer," Mark said as he stopped the car and got out.

A minute later they were in the sitting room. Mark was on the couch and she was sitting in a straight back chair. Georgia's head kept swiveling right and left as she took everything in. Mark was beginning to think this had been the wrong place to bring her. What was done was done, though, and if she had something to say, they had best get to it.

"We haven't had a chance to talk since...everything," he said, leaning forward.

She turned and gave him a blank look for a moment before seeming to pull herself together and focus on him instead of the things around them.

"Yes, well, that is partly my fault. I got your messages. I just wasn't up to talking. It was the strangest thing. All those nights I spent worrying that something was going to happen to him, and when something finally did I couldn't believe it."

Mark nodded. Grief struck people in different ways. And while Georgia had always been a cold, calculating woman, he did not doubt that she, too, had grieved in her own way.

"I'm sorry for your loss," he said.

"Thank you. I think you lost more than I did. Paul was your friend. I envied your closeness. He was always distant with me, never talked to me, told me things."

"Turns out that was how he was with everyone," Mark said grimly. "No one knew what was really going on his head. Who he really was," he paused. He wondered if Georgia had ever had cause to suspect that Paul wasn't who he claimed to be.

"Did anyone from the department ever contact you after his death?" he asked.

She shook her head. "Only you."

"Ah. What about his parents, sister, did you hear from them?"

"His sister was the one who called to tell me. I gather he had her listed as next of kin. Strange it would be her and not me."

"She was local in case of an emergency," Mark said, struggling to be tactful.

"You're right, of course. I got your message later that day."

"Did he ever talk to you about the time as a child when he was kidnapped?"

She blinked at him in surprise. "What an odd question. No, he never talked to me about it. Of course I knew about it. It was in the news when he was taken and again when he made his way home. I tried, once when we were dating and once more after we were married to get him to talk about it, but he refused. When I pushed he just got angry. It was more than that, though. It was like he was afraid."

"What of?"

"I don't honestly know, and I guess it doesn't matter now. I wanted to understand him, to know what he had gone through. Those are the kinds of things you're supposed to tell your spouse, aren't you?"

And for the first time since he'd known her, Mark actually felt sorry for her. Maybe some of the coldness she always radiated was a result of being in a marriage with someone who kept her at arm's length, wouldn't let her in. If Paul would have told anyone about what really happened to him, it would have been logical that she would have been the one.

But he hadn't.

Had Paul been afraid that if he told his wife the truth that she couldn't handle it, or that she'd tell his family? Or was there more? Was it possible he had been trying to protect her?

Paul was gone now, though, and the burden of his secrets fell on Mark's shoulders. As he sat there staring at Georgia, he debated about whether to tell her the truth. Would she refuse to accept it, like his parents, or would it reinforce her own feelings like it had with Paul's sister?

"Would you still want to know more about what happened to him?" he asked finally. He had to give her the choice. Some people when they lost someone were just as happy to be left in the dark about things they hadn't known so that they could remember the deceased as they had known them, and not as the stranger they had known so little about.

She slowly shook her head. "Sometimes knowledge can be a terrible burden. With Paul gone there's no reason I need to know about the things he wouldn't share with me. If we'd had children together I might feel differently, but I'm content to let his secrets stay buried along with him."

She didn't want to know. Whether or not she suspected she was at least quite clear that she didn't want to hear the truth.

"Fair enough. So, Georgia, if you're not looking for answers, what brings you out here. What can I do for you?"

"There's nothing you can do for me, Mark, but I'm pretty certain there's something I can do for you."

He found himself leaning forward, eager to hear whatever she was about to say next.

"About eight months after he died I was contacted by an attorney I had never heard of before. The man actually came to my apartment. He said he'd been retained by Paul years ago and in the event that Paul didn't check in with him for their yearly meeting then he was supposed to give this to me."

She pulled a small envelope out of her purse and handed it to Mark. He struggled to keep his hand from shaking as he reached for it. He could feel a tightening in his stomach as his hand closed on it. There was something important inside, he could feel it.

"Have you opened it?" he asked, having to clear his throat to get the words out.

"Yes. I studied the contents for days, but I finally gave up. I put the whole thing away. A couple of days ago I pulled it back out of my closet. I realized I could make no more sense of it now than I could then. That's when it occurred to me that I should give it to you. Maybe it will mean something to you. As it is, I'm done. I'm moving on with my life and I don't need anything from the old one holding me back. I'm sorry, that sounded really harsh. I didn't mean it that way. The truth is, I found someone and I'm getting remarried."

"Congratulations," Mark said.

"Thank you. It took me by surprise, actually. After my first marriage I just didn't think that marriage was for me. I've found a man that makes me feel different. He's French, actually. I must admit the whole thing has been a bit overwhelming. But you see now why I felt the need to give this to you, to close that chapter so I can begin a new one?"

Mark nodded, barely hearing her as he slowly opened the envelope. Inside there were two items. The first was a single sheet of paper with some unintelligible writing on it that was in Paul's handwriting. He frowned as he stared at it. It looked like some sort of code. The second item was a small brass key.

Before he could say anything, Georgia spoke up. "I have no idea what the key goes to and whatever he wrote it just looks like gibberish to me. Honestly, I can't even figure out why he bothered to have this sent on by that attorney."

He wanted this to go to someone in case he died. It was a contingency plan, a safety net, Mark thought to himself. He wished he'd had the paper and key back when Georgia first received them, but it was okay. He'd do what he could with them now.

"Do you have the attorney's name and contact information?" he asked.

She nodded and pulled a business card out of her purse which she handed to him. "I kept it in case I ever figured out what it all meant or I needed to ask him something," she said. "I'm glad to be rid of it all. It kind of disturbed me, there was something almost sinister feeling about it."

"Was there anything else the attorney told you?"

"Not that I can think of."

"If I find what this key goes to, what it all means-"

She reached out and gripped his hand, cutting him off. "Mark, I know I have no right to ask this of you, to make my burden yours, but I couldn't bring myself to throw this away. For whatever reason it was important enough for

Paul to arrange for it to come to me. The truth is, though, I don't want to know. I stopped trying to solve the mystery that was my husband the day I left for New York. Whatever you find, I don't care what it is, I don't want to know, and I don't want to lay any claim to it. If it's money, I have enough of my own. If it's personal papers, I'm sure you can figure out what best to do with them."

"You really want out, don't you?"

"More than I can tell you," she said, and he could actually see tears sparkling in her eyes. "I tried...I tried and it made me crazy. I can't go back to crazy, Mark."

He had felt like that himself on more than one occasion since discovering that Paul had been an imposter. He chose his next words with care. He owed that to Paul, if not to Georgia.

"I will do everything in my power to keep you out of anything that I find. I'm sorry for what you went through, and I wish you nothing but good luck and happiness with this new man."

"Thank you, Mark, that actually means more to me than you can guess. It's the closest I could ever come to feeling like I had Paul's blessing. I did love him, you know, as distant and impossible and frustrating as he was. I don't know if he ever told you, but he respected you deeply. I think you're the only one he respected of all those in his life. More than once he told me that you were a truly good man and that those were hard to find."

Mark was caught unprepared for the wave of emotion that suddenly rocked him. "I appreciate that," he managed to get out around the sudden lump in his throat.

"He said that the thing he liked best about you was that you could always be trusted to do the right thing."

And just like that Mark felt like he was back in the police station, just outside the interrogation room where Paul told him he was going up to Green Pastures to try and stop the assassins who were after Jeremiah and the kids. Mark had asked him what he should do. He'd never forget the look in Paul's eyes or the last words he'd said to him.

You're a good cop, Mark. The best. Inside that room is a man who is your prisoner. And he's the only one who can call off a team of killers who are about to slaughter fourteen kids and a rabbi. If they haven't already. Do whatever you feel led to do.

Those words had haunted him for so long. He'd always suspected that Paul knew what he would do, was urging him to torture the guy they were holding into calling off the attack. What Georgia had just said confirmed that for him. Paul believed he would always do the right thing.

By many people's standards what Mark had done had been the wrong thing. Before he could return to active duty as a police officer he'd had to come to terms with himself and the fact that he still wasn't convinced he'd been wrong, even if his actions had ultimately proven futile.

"Do you... do you know what any of this is?" Georgia asked hesitantly, indicating the paper and the key.

"No, but I have my suspicions about what they might pertain to."

She nodded slowly. "See, this is the dangerous part. Curiosity. It doesn't just kill cats. In my case it killed my marriage. I liked that the man I was marrying had an air of mystery to him, that he was a riddle I thought I could solve. When I couldn't, when he wouldn't let me even try...well, you know what happened. The sad thing is that he's been dead for almost two years and here I am...still trying."

She shook her head resolutely. "That's why I have to be done with all of this. With him. Do you understand?" Her voice was pleading at the end, like she needed him to give her permission to walk away.

"More than you can know. And if it helps, as far as I can tell, he never let anyone in when he was alive. He's just left us all to try and figure it out afterward."

"That actually does make me feel better. I figured if there was one person he would have confided in, it was you. I was always quite jealous of you because of that. I'm sorry. I know it was childish. That's why I said no to so many chances to have dinner with you and your wife."

"Traci will be relieved to hear that. She always thought it was her cooking," Mark joked, trying to bring the mood up a little before they both ended up blubbering.

Georgia laughed. "Tell her I'm sorry, that it had nothing to do with her. She's a lovely woman. And she was always the perfect wife for a detective. Something I, alas, was not."

"So she won't get a big head about it I'll make sure to point out that it's because she has a perfect detective for a husband."

Georgia cocked her head and regarded him quizzically for a moment. "You know, you've changed. You're more personable, less abrasive than you use to be."

"Thanks."

"I'm sorry, that wasn't a nice thing to say. I guess I'm just stressed enough that I'm saying whatever comes to mind."

"We've both changed because of Paul, because of what happened to him and because of the things that have happened to us because of it or despite of it. I've made some close friends who've helped me get through. And I'm a father now. Traci and I had twins over the summer."

"Congratulations!" she said, her face lighting up. "Oh, I bet Traci makes the most adorable mother."

"So adorable it's ridiculous!"

"Paul was always very adamant about not wanting kids," she said, suddenly wistful. "It never made sense either. He had nice parents, a good upbringing, but he was just dead set against it."

Mark shrugged. "Well, it's not too late. Looks like you're getting a second chance at a happy family."

"I do hope so." She glanced at her watch. "I need to be going. I have a plane to catch back home. I just didn't feel right mailing things off. I wanted to know that you got them. And I guess, I needed some more closure with Paul and being able to talk it through with you was the next best thing. Silly, I know."

She stood and nervously smoothed down her skirt. Mark rose as well.

"Not at all. Listen, I know we were never close, but if there's anything you need, please call."

"Thank you. Please don't take this the wrong way, but I hope I never have to."

He nodded. "Don't worry about it."

The feeling, after all, was entirely mutual. They did share a connection because in one way or another Paul and his secrets had messed up both their lives, but at the end of the day that was all they had in common.

"Would you like me to take you to the airport?"

"No, I've already taken up too much of your time. The taxi driver who dropped me off at your office is going to be picking me up there in a few minutes."

"Well, then let's get you back there," Mark said.

As he locked up and set the alarm Georgia took one last admiring look at the house. "The Coulters must be even richer than I had heard. Wait until I tell everyone I saw the inside of their house."

It was nice to know that despite the fact that they'd had a moment of growth and connection that she was still just as shallow as he'd always figured her to be. It meant he didn't have to rethink everything about her.

The ride back to police headquarters was a quiet one. They'd both run out of things to say to each other, but that was fine. She was probably looking ahead to her new life while he was busy thinking back on Paul's old one.

One thing was for sure, she had dropped a whole new can of worms in his lap. He'd just about reached a place where he was thinking of letting the past go. He had two beautiful children to focus every moment of free time on now and he'd at least answered some of the most basic questions surrounding who his old friend and partner had really been.

Deep down, though, he'd always known that he wasn't done with Paul, or Not Paul, as he and Traci had come to call him privately. Even though he knew now that Not Paul's birth name had been Andrew, Mark still had a problem calling him that.

When they pulled into the parking lot, Georgia's taxi was waiting for her.

"Thank you, for everything," she said, before getting out of the car.

"Remember, if you need me just call," he said.

She nodded and closed the door before heading off to her cab.

Mark turned off the engine and watched as the taxi drove out of sight. Then he fished the business card she'd given him for the attorney out of the envelope with the other items.

Kent Gordon was the name of the man Paul had entrusted the envelope with. Mark just hoped he'd have some answers for him. The law firm was located up in northern California and it looked like Kent was one of the named partners. So, what had Paul told the man that had compelled a partner in a law firm to fly all the way across country to deliver a package to Georgia? He dialed the number for the Mitchell and Gordon law firm and when a woman answered the phone he asked for Kent Gordon.

"Hold please," she said, her voice suddenly tense.

Before he could respond she'd put him on hold, listening to what was some of the most tinny elevator music he'd ever heard. A minute later a man answered the phone. "This is Fred Mitchell, can I help you?"

"Actually, I was trying to reach Kent Gordon," Mark said.

"Mr. Gordon is no longer with the firm. Were you a client of his?"

"Actually no, but a friend of mine was and I need some information that only Gordon can give me. My name is Detective Mark Walters, I'm with the Pine Springs police department."

"Then I regret to inform you, Detective, that you won't be getting any information out of Kent Gordon."

"And why is that exactly?"

"He was killed a little over a year ago."

3

"Hello, Detective? Are you still there?"

Mark's mind was racing as he tried to process the news that the man who had carried out Paul's last wishes was dead. He shook his head and forced himself to speak. "I'm sorry for your loss. Do you mind telling me how Kent Gordon was killed?"

"Car accident. It was the blasted fog that got him. Went right off the road."

"I see."

"Is there anything I can help you with, Detective?"

"There might be. It involved a client of his who is also deceased."

"If you give me the name I can have my secretary pull the files."

Mark hesitated. There was no reason. There was nothing about Fred Mitchell that seemed out of place. And fog made for incredibly hazardous driving conditions. Still, something felt slightly off about the whole thing to him.

"His name was Paul Dryer."

"I'll have her get the files and I'll call you back Tuesday to discuss. What number can I reach you on?"

Mark gave the man his cell number before hanging up. He sat in the car for a moment, trying to gather his thoughts. It was late afternoon. He could go back inside and stare at papers without reading them for another half hour. He started the car and headed out of the parking lot, deciding that going home sounded like a better plan.

When he walked through the door Traci handed him both babies before throwing herself down on the couch, gesturing dramatically.

"No need to ask how your day was," he said drily as he juggled his son and daughter.

"The other mothers at the park make it look so easy," Traci said.

"The other mothers aren't juggling two hellions at once."

"No, you're right. One of them was juggling three."

"Triplets, I can't even imagine."

"Neither can I," Traci said, struggling to sit up. In the last seven months she'd lost all her baby weight and then some. She looked thin and tired.

"Do you want me to make dinner tonight?" he asked.

"Only if it means making a reservation and getting a sitter."

"You know what? I've had an interesting day, too. That's probably not a bad idea. Who should I call? Your sister and brother-in-law?"

"The whole family is sick over there, plus I don't want to have to drive all the way out to their place to have to drive all the way back. How about Joseph and Geanie?"

"I kind of imposed on Joseph earlier."

"Okay, your day has been interesting," Traci said.

"Still, they have said any time..."

"Now, right now, is any time."

"You want to hold the babies while I call?" Mark asked, arms quickly tiring.

"No. I'll call. You can get them ready to go in the car."

"Better yet, see if they can come here."

"I like the way you think, Detective," Traci said as she retrieved her cell from her purse.

"It's a good thing you married me then."

Cindy didn't know why she was so nervous. She had dumped the entire contents of her closet onto her bed at some point. Half of the clothes had slid onto the floor and she kept trying to step over them but kept stepping on them as she made her way around the room. At one point she got a foot twisted up in a sweater and fell. Fortunately she landed on the bed. Unfortunately a metal hanger dug into her side and she winced in pain even as she hoped it didn't leave a bruise.

She had called Geanie half an hour before for help only to find out that she and Joseph were babysitting the twins. Geanie hadn't even answered her phone. It had been Joseph who picked up and let her know what was going on. Cindy wasn't sure if the screaming laughter she'd heard in the background had been coming from the kids or from Geanie.

She didn't have Geanie or Traci or even Joseph to call on in her moment of crisis and she lay on the bed in disgust, the hanger still digging into her side.

"I need more friends," she muttered.

She managed to push herself to her feet, extricate herself from the sweater, and stagger out of the room. She grabbed her phone and called the only person she had left that she could think of to call.

"Hello?" Dave answered.

The youth pastor, affectionately known by almost everyone as Wildman, sounded tired and a little down.

"Wildman, I need your help," she said. "I'm desperate."

"Cindy? What on earth is wrong?" he asked.

"Everything. Nothing." She sat down on the couch with a sigh. "It's complicated. Do you have a few minutes to help?"

There was a pause and then he said, "Sure, I could use the distraction."

In the back of her mind tiny alarm bells went off. Dave had been acting strangely since just before Christmas. "Are you okay?"

"Fine. What is it you need?"

"Well, I'm going undercover at a couples' retreat to try and find out what happened to a guy who went missing. Jeremiah and I have to act like a couple. We leave Sunday, and I'm just totally lost at the moment."

"About how to act like a couple? That shouldn't be too hard."

"No! I mean, it will be, I mean, never mind. That's not my problem right now."

"Then what on earth is your problem?" he asked, sounding bewildered.

"I don't know what to wear."

"Are you kidding?"

"Of course I'm not kidding! This is a real problem. I figured you were married so you would understand."

He grunted in reply. She had no idea what that was supposed to mean so she pressed on.

"I want to wear something alluring. I mean, I'm pretending to be in a couple working on our relationship."

"So, you want something sexy?"

She felt herself flush just hearing him use that word. "Not sexy, appealing, attractive."

"Sexy."

"No! I want something that will capture someone's attention."

"Like Jeremiah?"

"Well, yes, he will be playing my...boyfriend," she said, choking a bit on the word. "And I want to make sure that I look like a woman who's actually trying. I want to look, I don't know."

"Sexy."

"Okay, fine! I want to look sexy!" she said, embarrassed to say it out loud.

"At least now you're being honest."

"But not slutty or anything like that."

"Cindy, there's about a thousand miles between those two things. Most women don't realize it because they don't really get men and how we think. I'm always counseling some of the teen girls who think they're trying to be attractive and mature and instead are just making themselves look cheap and insecure."

Cindy leaned her head back with a sigh. "I think I might be one of those teenage girls."

"I've never seen you wear anything cheap or slutty looking."

"Yeah, but have you ever seen me wear anything sexy? I'm pretty sure I don't know how."

Dave sighed audibly on the other end of the line. "Maybe you should be having this conversation with your father. My father helped all my sisters through this transition in their lives. Granted, they were all younger than you are, but still."

"I'm not having this conversation with my father."

"Your brother?"

"No."

"And I'm guessing as the object of your sexy intentions Jeremiah is right out."

"Yes!" she said, horrified at the suggestion. "Please, Dave. I need help. There's no one else I can call right now. I trust you."

"That's your first mistake. All guys think about sex. A lot. It's in our physiology."

"Dave!"

"Hey, you came to a youth pastor for help. You think I don't have to have blunt talks with kids all the time who don't know what to do with all these new urges and desires? Trust me, I wish all parents did a great job of dealing with this, but the truth is most of them are too embarrassed to have honest conversations with their kid. So they go into denial about it. You know I once had to have one of the female counselors go with a junior high girl to the store to help her buy her first bra because her mother was in denial that she was old enough to need one?"

"That's terrible!"

"You're telling me! I was the one the girl started sobbing on because she didn't know who else to tell. The things she said can never be unheard. But, that's my job. Kids are raw, honest. They haven't learned to hide their feelings as well or that there are some things that are just not appropriate to say at certain times. You know a high school kid's brain has more in common with the brain of a toddler than the brain of a college student? Very little impulse control."

"I had no idea."

"Yeah, hazards of the job. Look, if you need my help, you've got it."

"Thank you. Could you come over and help me pack?"

"No."

"No? Why not?"

"Cindy. Between work and church I've seen all your clothes. Unless you're hiding some crazy things in the back of your closet none of it is going to work for what you want."

"Well, what am I supposed to do?" she asked, struggling with the fact that she felt a bit embarrassed. She took a deep breath and reminded herself that she had nothing to be embarrassed about. Her clothes were neat, nice, and completely appropriate.

For church.

Because for years that had been her entire world.

"I'll meet you at the mall in half an hour. Be outside Trendies. Bring your credit card and wear pantyhose."

He hung up and she sat for a moment, wondering if calling him had been a huge mistake. Her finger hovered over his name, ready to call him back and tell him to forget it, that she'd make do with what she had.

She took a deep breath. She had asked him. She was responsible for opening Pandora's box. Now it was time to deal with the consequences.

When she arrived outside Trendies half an hour later Dave was already waiting for her. He smiled when he saw her, but it didn't reach his eyes. There was something going on with him, but he really didn't seem to want to talk about it. Now was probably not the time to push, though. They were in a public place and she needed his help so she couldn't risk alienating him.

"You ever been in here?" he asked.

"No."

"Why?"

"I guess the name kind of scared me off," she admitted. "I'm not exactly a fashion follower."

"Neither is Trendies. It's a fashion creator. More than that it's an eclectic blend of old and new. Whatever your style, you'll find things in here for you."

"How do you know so much?" she asked.

He rolled his eyes. "Youth pastor. I know more about most things than I want to. Last year three of our girls who attend Christian high schools asked me to come homecoming dress shopping with them to make sure their dresses would conform to the school's decency standards. I'll never get those five hours of my life back, I'll tell you."

"I thought you loved being a youth pastor, dealing with the kids."

"The kids, yes. Some of the drama, no."

She followed him into the store which had a warehouse kind of vibe to it, complete with a second floor that had a catwalk criss-crossing overhead. Everywhere she looked there were racks and racks of clothes representing so many different styles and decades that it boggled her mind. "Are these consignment clothes?" she asked.

"Nope, they just look vintage. Everything is new, made for this store. It's what they're known for."

"I don't even know where to begin," she admitted.

"How long are you going to be gone?"

"It could be six days, although hopefully we'll find what we have to and be out of there before then."

"Did they give you any kind of itinerary?"

34

"No, I just know it's some sort of retreat to promote intimacy."

Dave actually smirked at that. "Oh, you're going to have a good time. I'd pay money to see which of you freaks out and blows your cover first." He chuckled and he seemed suddenly more like himself. "So, tell you what, let's try to make Jeremiah blink first in this game of chicken you'll be playing with him," he said.

His eyes were sparkling now and he seemed to be thoroughly enjoying himself.

"I'm not sure I like where your mind is going."

"Oh, trust me, Jeremiah will."

"What do you have in mind?"

"Cindy, we're going to show him a whole new side of you. And it's going to drive him bananas."

She found herself starting to smile at the thought. She wouldn't mind driving Jeremiah a little crazy. Ever since Israel he had been subdued around her most of the time and it was becoming irritating. Shaking him up a little might be just what the doctor ordered.

"Where do we start?"

"Where all women's wardrobes should start. With the perfect little, black dress."

"I have a little, black dress," she protested.

He rolled his eyes at her. "You have a dress you wear to funerals. I saw it. At a funeral. That's not a little, black dress. That's a tragedy that you wear to appropriately tragic occasions."

"Ouch."

"You wanted tactful-"

"I should have called someone else. I get it."

"Okay, then let's get down to business. You'll have to try on a few of them until we get the sense of what works best with your figure."

"Don't you already know?" she asked, unable to keep a hint of sarcasm out of her voice.

"I make it a point not to look at other women's figures. Besides, with the clothes you wear I wouldn't have been able to guess even if I had been looking."

She punched him lightly in the shoulder. It was the only appropriate response she could think of. "Don't hurt my feelings," she threatened.

"I'm not trying to. I'm just saying that you've never been in the business of attracting the opposite sex. There's nothing wrong with that, but you're going to need to go at things completely differently than you have been. Fortunately for you Jeremiah is already head over heels about you. A little tweak here and there and he probably won't be able to keep his hands off you."

She felt herself flushing all the way to the roots of her hair.

"Don't worry. I know you're crazy about him, too. My lips are sealed, though."

"Thank you. For everything."

He smiled and patted her on the arm. "You're welcome. Actually, I should be the one thanking you. I've been feeling pretty useless lately and this is great."

Before she could question him he turned and started pointing to a couple of different racks. "Grab your size and head to the dressing room. I'll be prowling around. Holler when you're ready to model."

Cindy grabbed the dresses he had indicated and headed for the dressing room. She'd never actually modeled clothes for a man before and she felt a little self-conscious as she walked out in the first dress, a halter top with a full but very short skirt.

"Turn for me," he said.

She did a little turn, feeling even more self-conscious.

"Okay, try the next one," he said.

She went through four black dresses before he had selected the one he thought she should get. It was form fitting with a sweetheart neckline that she was grateful only revealed the barest hint of cleavage. The shoulder strap mini sleeve things which she wasn't exactly sure what to call angled outward on her shoulders. It was just shy of being an off-the-shoulder dress. It hugged her waist and hips tight and the skirt ended about three inches above her knee. It was shorter than she was used to, but not so short that she felt uncomfortable.

"There, that is perfection," Dave declared with a satisfied nod.

She looked down at herself. She looked good, and the dress fit really well, but she wasn't sure what made it better than a couple of the others. "Can I ask what makes this one sexier than some of the others?"

He nodded. "The neckline for one. The sweetheart neck emphasizes your natural assets. It shows barely any cleavage, just enough so that a guy can't help but notice, but not enough to make it feel like you're advertising. Then the angle of the straps emphasizes your collarbones and you have nice ones, along with very feminine shoulders. Form fitting around the hips and waist are great if your stomach is mostly flat which yours is. Finally, the hemline hits you in a perfect spot. If you were taller or shorter it wouldn't, but where it hits really helps elongate your legs.

THOU ART WITH ME

Guys like to see legs and like to feel that they're nice and long, but if you have a hemline that's too high it's not good. A bit of a tease is always better than a full reveal."

"And here I assumed guys just wanted us wearing less material all over."

"Not unless you're talking about a bathing suit, which we will deal with later. No, sexy elegant is always better than slutty trashy, at least for any type of man you'd want to attract. You need to leave some mystery to yourself when you dress. It's more tantalizing and it also gets you more respect. I know, it seems counter-intuitive, but it's true."

"I feel like I should be taking notes," she joked.

He nodded. "Maybe so, because I'm going to let you try picking out the next two dresses. We want one that's white and one that's red. Then we'll move on to daywear, swimsuits, all that kind of stuff. We'll get you some shoes, too."

"I'm not sure I can afford all this."

He smiled. "Another one of the reasons why this store is so popular? The prices are cheap enough it will shock you. We'll work it out, don't worry."

It took another two hours but when they were done Cindy had enough clothes for the trip and it didn't break the bank. She thanked Dave and headed home. As she neared her house she realized that she was singing softly to herself. She smiled. Sometimes all a girl needed was a good shopping spree.

She turned onto her street and a moment later pulled up to her house only to be surprised to see Jeremiah's car in her driveway. She parked next to him and got out. He wasn't in the car and he wasn't on the porch. She could see that the lights were on in her living room, though, and she was pretty sure she had turned them off when she left.

Cautiously she approached the front door. It was unlocked.

She opened it.

"Hello?" she called, hesitant to go any further until she knew for sure what she was walking into.

Jeremiah appeared from the kitchen, a frown on his face. "You weren't picking up your phone," he said.

"Sorry. I was out shopping and I didn't hear it. What's wrong?"

"We need to talk."

4

Cindy was pretty sure that there was no one on the planet who enjoyed hearing those words 'we need to talk'. She knew she certainly didn't feel good after hearing Jeremiah say them.

"Should I sit down?" she asked as she closed the front door.

"Yeah, come in," he said as though inviting her into his home instead of her own.

"Thanks," she said drily as she moved into the living room and took a seat on the couch.

Jeremiah stood in front of her, forehead wrinkled in concern. "I worried when you weren't answering your phone. I let myself in."

She nodded, not bothering to comment on the fact that he must have picked the lock.

"I could tell that you were busy trying to pack for the trip," he continued.

"Yeah, sorry, the place is a bit of a mess."

"It's okay. Mine's in a bit of chaos as well."

She very much doubted that he had the entire contents of his closet strewn around his room, but she refrained from saying that. "Jeremiah, why are you here?"

He took a deep breath. "I realized that we needed to get our stories straight for the retreat and lay some ground rules before we get there."

"Oh, okay," she said, relaxing somewhat. "So, where do you want to start?"

"Well, they'll likely ask us personal questions and we should be on the same page and remember what we're saying so it doesn't throw up any red flags. We are there undercover after all, and we don't want that cover blown."

She nodded as she realized that he must be used to doing undercover work. She hadn't even really given much thought to what backstory they were going to give to the people at the retreat center. Once he said something, though, she realized that it would be important to have a consistent story.

"So, how long have we been together?" he asked.

She felt her breath catch slightly in her throat. "You tell me."

"Okay. We've known each other for about two years, but we got serious over the summer."

"That should be easy enough to remember," she said drily.

"Obviously there are some issues we're working through in our relationship. We both have different religions for one and that's hard on us and our families."

"That would be an understatement on the part of your family, at least."

"Exactly. The key to a successful cover story is weaving just enough fact in there to make it believable and to help you keep it straight. I had Mark register us as Cindy Prescott and Jeremiah Goldsmith. We keep our own first names."

"Well, one of us does at least," she said, alluding to the fact that Jeremiah was already a false name.

He ignored her comment and continued. "We're from northern California, Castro Valley in the Bay Area. It's small enough that not all southern Californians have heard of it. We're coming down here because we wanted to get away from family, friends, jobs, everything so we could just focus on us."

"And why are we focusing on just us? Why do we need a couples' retreat?"

"Obviously there's been a lot of stress, pressure, cultural differences. We're needing a retreat so we can figure out if this is going to work between us."

Again she felt her breath catch in her throat. Was that part of the cover story or the truth? Then again, as he had told her, good cover stories had as much of the truth in them as possible.

"Sounds reasonable," she forced herself to say. She hesitated a moment then continued on. "Just how physical are we as a couple? I mean, that's bound to come up."

He frowned as though thinking. "Not very. I mean we hold hands and kiss, but not a whole lot and certainly nothing more."

"Why?"

"Because you're religious, obviously."

"And you're not?" she asked, raising an eyebrow.

"Well, of course, but it's usually more realistic for the girl to dictate the level of intimacy in these things."

"Is it?" she asked.

"Yes, of course. Why?"

"Oh, just asking. I wouldn't know, you see. I've never had a serious relationship before."

"That's good. We'll leave that in. It can help with some of the conflicted emotions we'll be there to work through."

Cindy stared at him wondering if he was an idiot or just pretending to be an idiot. As no answer seemed forthcoming she asked a new question. "What are we planning on naming our kids if things go that way? Most serious couples talk about things like that. At least, I assume they do."

"We don't talk about that."

"Then maybe one of us is less serious than the other and having commitment issues."

"Let's try not to get too complicated with our cover stories. We need things that are easy to remember. The more we bog down with details the more likely one of us is to slip up."

And from the tone of his voice and the look in his eyes she was pretty sure she knew which one of them he was worried was going to slip up.

"Okay, keeping it simple," she said.

"Excellent."

"Now that we've got that sorted out, do we have a plan for finding this missing friend of the captain's?"

"We'll have to keep our eyes and ears open, obviously, for anything suspicious. When we have a chance to slip away unobserved we can do some snooping around, maybe even break into the office and check for any records on him or his stay. Hopefully we can get a member of the staff to talk as well, start with a casual name dropping, and see where that leads us.

Casual. Cindy had a feeling that there was going to be absolutely nothing casual about this trip, including the "casual" daywear Dave had helped her pick out.

As if reading her mind he suddenly asked, "What were you shopping for?"

"Oh, you know, toiletries and such. A few things for the trip," she said quickly, not wanting to give away the surprise. Fortunately, she'd left her bags in the trunk.

"Okay. Are you sure you're up to this? With everything that's happened...and I know undercover work is hard even for those trained for it."

"I'll be fine," she said, trying to put as much confidence into her voice as possible.

"Good. Do you have any questions?"

"Yes, actually, I've had something I wanted to ask you all day."

"What is it?"

"What was going on when I came into the office and you said Marie said you should think about marrying me?"

"Oh, that. She was expressing concern about me and the fact that I haven't found a nice Jewish woman to settle down with. She asked me to give serious consideration to marrying the next single woman who walked into the office."

"And that just happened to be me?"

"Yes. Crazy, isn't it?"

That wasn't the word she would have chosen, but she was willing to let it go.

"Is there anything else we need to discuss?" she asked, feeling suddenly very, very tired.

Jeremiah was worried. He wasn't sure Cindy realized the full extent of the potential danger they were walking into. A man was missing and once they were at the retreat center they would be effectively cut off from the outside world and help. Maintaining a cover for a couple of hours or a day was one thing. Maintaining a cover for a week while under relentless scrutiny from people whose sole job was to work with couples and help them improve their relationship was another thing entirely. If they weren't careful they could be found out in a heartbeat. Until they'd had a chance to do some investigating, they'd have no idea who might be involved. There would be no one to trust, no opportunity to let their guard down.

"Are you okay?" Cindy asked.

"Yes. I'm just concerned about the risk we're taking."

"It will be fine. We've been in so many worse situations."

He wasn't sure if she actually believed that or if she was just trying to be upbeat.

"Cindy. This is going to be dangerous. We don't have to do this. We can tell Mark that we've changed our minds."

She shook her head. "We owe it to Mark. Besides a guy is missing and maybe we can help find him before he ends up dead."

Jeremiah very much doubted that. It was difficult to keep a grown man prisoner for any length of time without proper facilities and personnel to pull it off. It was dangerous, too, as there was always risk of discovery. No, he was pretty sure that whatever had happened to the man, he was already dead. The best they could hope to do was find out why and see the killer brought to justice.

Cindy was looking tired and frustrated. She was also distracted. She probably wanted to finish packing without him around getting in the way.

"Is there anything I can do to help you get ready?" he asked, guessing that she would say "no".

"You've already done more than enough," she said with a tight smile.

"Okay, I'll see you in the morning then. Call if you need anything."

"Okay."

He left. Cindy was acting a bit odd, but he didn't have time to worry about that right now. He had to go home and figure out exactly what he should pack. A gun, as much as he wanted to bring one, was probably out of the question. Here he was just a regular citizen, even if he was being sent in undercover somewhere.

He toyed with the possibility of getting a concealed weapons permit, but that would not help him fly under the radar. Just because the people closest to him knew his secret didn't mean he wasn't still essentially hiding his true identity and attempting to do so for the rest of his life. He sighed. Why did things have to be so complicated?

After Jeremiah drove off Cindy got her bags out of her trunk. She threw what she could in the washing machine and went into her bedroom to grab her suitcase. It really did look like a bomb had gone off in the room and she stared for a moment, disgusted, as she thought about how much work it was going to be to put it all back, particularly since none of it was going with her.

Suddenly the pile of clothes on the bed moved. Cindy backpedaled quickly, heart pounding as someone or something seemed to be rising from their hiding place.

Cindy felt an intense surge of relief as a tiny black head popped out of the pile of clothes. Sleepy yellow eyes blinked at her.

"Blackie! How long have you been in there?"

The kitten yawned and stretched before sauntering over to her. She shouldn't have been surprised. He loved to tunnel under anything and everything he possibly could. She sat down on top of the pile of clothes and he climbed into her lap, purring his heart out.

"You're going to get to stay with Aunt Geanie and Uncle Joseph for a few days," she told him. "Aunt Geanie will pick you up after work tomorrow."

She had to feel a little sorry for Geanie and Joseph. They had somehow become the go-to babysitters for all the kids and pets in their little circle. At least they didn't seem to mind. Jeremiah's dog would be going there, too. Captain and Blackie had become good friends. The big German Shepherd seemed to think that the tiny kitten was his responsibility. Joseph's poodle was so well-mannered that she had no more than sniffed Blackie once when they were first introduced and then promptly ignored the mischievous kitten. So, no worries there. Cindy did have one other concern, though.

"Just don't get lost in their big house and make everyone have to go look for you," Cindy admonished.

Blackie closed his eyes, clearly making no promises.

The next couple days sped by and Cindy woke Monday morning with butterflies in her stomach. She was far more nervous than she had thought she would be. She put on a new white pencil skirt that was shorter than the little black dress and paired it with a sleeveless, pink blouse of raw silk. She slid on a new pair of pink pumps. After fluffing her hair and putting on some make-up she squared her shoulders as she faced herself in the mirror.

"You can do this," she told her reflection. "Find the bad guys, save the day, wow the guy. You totally can do this."

She heard a car pull up outside. That would be Mark come to pick her up. She took a deep breath, walked into the family room, grabbed her bags and headed out.

Jeremiah was already in the backseat and she hesitated.

"Love birds sit together in the back," Mark said as he helped her put her luggage in the trunk. "Just pretend I'm your chauffer."

"Should we call you James?" she asked, smirking.

"Do and I'll turn this car right around," he threatened.

Moments later she was in the backseat. Jeremiah quietly reached out and grabbed her hand, surprising her slightly. She gave it a squeeze, expecting him to let go, but he held on.

"New outfit?" he asked.

"Yes, do you like it?"

"It's very nice."

They were on the road in a minute.

"Okay, my captain's friend who went missing was named Malcolm Griffith. Here's a picture," Mark said, passing a photograph back to them.

He was an older looking man, with salt and pepper hair but he looked extremely fit. He looked like the type who was into healthy living, jogging, and all that.

"He went missing a week ago. He was at a health and wellness retreat by himself. Every six months or so he does one of those. Detox, destress, all that stuff," Mark said. "He never came home, and his wife is frantic. Now the center claims to have no knowledge of what happened to him."

"Do we know when exactly he disappeared?" Cindy asked.

"Not with one hundred percent certainty. He was in the habit of phoning his wife twice a day during these retreats and sending her pictures all throughout the day showing him doing whatever. On the fourth day of a seven day retreat he never checked in. That evening she called over there and was told that he was in a treatment session and couldn't be disturbed. She got the same thing on the fifth day and on the sixth they said he wasn't there, but that they didn't know where he'd gone."

"Poor woman," Cindy said. "It would be terrible not to know what had happened, waiting to hear something, anything."

"Well, hopefully we can give her some closure. The captain's hoping for a happy ending, but I'm not holding out much hope of that myself. Now I want you to check in twice a day with me. If you miss a check in I'll be on my way out as fast as I can. Remember, you're at a resort, but you're not exactly on American soil anymore. Tread carefully."

"Anything else?" Jeremiah asked quietly.

Mark glanced in the rear view mirror. "Yes, for goodness sake, take the time to figure out what the deal is with you two. It would save us all a lot of grief."

THOU ART WITH ME

5

Mark couldn't help but wonder as they drove which one of the three of them was going to explode first. The tension in the car was palpable. He knew why he was about ready to have a fit, but he didn't know exactly what was up with the other two. It had that relationship weirdness vibe to it. Actually that was probably a good thing given where they were headed. There was no way people wouldn't think they were a couple.

The drive took a little less than two hours. When they reached the tribal lands the first structure they passed was a tourist center. The second was a large casino with an attached hotel. A couple miles past that they found the retreat center.

Mark couldn't help but think it looked just like you would expect. Trees, a fountain, all designed to look like a little oasis where the buildings were all one story and placed so as to not intrude on the landscape. Isolated. A nice place to kill someone and get away with it.

"It's not too late to tell my boss where to go," Mark said.

"We're here. We'll do it," Cindy told him.

Mark pulled to a stop in front of the main building. "Be careful," he said, voice low.

"We will," Jeremiah assured him before getting out of the car. Mark popped the trunk and climbed out as well to help with the bags. He couldn't shake his feeling of unease at the idea of leaving his friends here. He told himself he was being ridiculous. Jeremiah was more than capable of handling anything that might come at them.

Maybe it was all the feelings about Paul and his death that had been dredged up again that was making him loathe to let the rabbi and the secretary out of his sight. After the bags were out of the trunk, he startled all three of them by giving them quick hugs before getting back in the car.

As he drove off he kept glancing back in the rearview mirror until they were lost to sight. He should have told Cindy to send up an extra prayer for their safety from him.

Cindy couldn't contain a little thrill of excitement as she and Jeremiah stepped up to the front desk to check in. Even as she felt it she realized that what she should be feeling was fear or trepidation. Sometimes it hit her just how different she was now than when she and Jeremiah had first met. She wasn't frightened as easily. She took risks. More than all of that, though, the feelings that Jeremiah had stirred within her were the most miraculous change of all.

"Are you okay?" Jeremiah asked quietly.

"I am," she said, unable to suppress a sudden smile. She, for one, planned on taking Mark's advice to heart that she and Jeremiah use the time to figure things out. With the wardrobe that Dave had helped her choose in her luggage she was feeling pretty confident that she'd have Jeremiah's full attention while talking things through.

She did feel a moment of trepidation as Jeremiah handed over the fake driver's licenses that Mark had provided with their assumed names on them. The woman behind the desk didn't even give them a second glance, though.

"I have you booked in a room with two double beds," she informed Cindy and Jeremiah. "Do you want me to see if I can find an available room with a queen?"

"No, the two doubles is good," Jeremiah said.

"Okay, then you're all set in bungalow 14," she told them, handing Jeremiah two keys along with some paperwork. "Everything you need to know is in there, including your schedule and a map," she instructed them. "There is an afternoon meet and greet followed by dinner with your instructors and fellow attendees. To get to your room you go out these doors on my left, take a right and it will be the last bungalow."

"Thank you," Jeremiah said.

They grabbed their bags and headed for the bungalow. As they walked Cindy tried to take everything in. It seemed like out of the doors there were bungalows in both directions. Arrows on the walls showed that 1-14 were on the right, 15-28 were on the left and straight ahead somewhere in the gardens were 29 and 30. She wondered if those two were larger, like suites, and that was why they were separate.

The bungalows were spaced out enough to give everyone a bit of privacy, feel like they were in their own oasis without having the neighbors right there sharing a wall or even a view. It would make it easier for her and Jeremiah to talk freely when they were in theirs, but it would also make it harder for them to spy on their neighbors.

Of course, it was unlikely that their neighbors, fellow retreat attendees, would need spying on. They wouldn't have been there when Malcolm was there. No, it would be the staffers that they would need to spy on.

It took them a couple of minutes to walk to their bungalow. Once inside Cindy quickly moved to take the bed closest to the bathroom, leaving Jeremiah the bed near the sliding glass doors that led to a little outdoor sitting area. The room was done up in white with an occasional touch of tan, making it very plain.

"Not a lot to look at," she commented as she put her bag in the closet.

"I think that's the point. They don't want anything that will be a distraction to those staying here. You know, clear people's minds, minimize the clutter, and the chaos."

"And the color," she added drily.

She noted there wasn't a television in the room either. At a couples' retreat that was probably a good thing, forcing people to talk to each other instead of stare mindlessly at the television when they got back to their rooms. Aside from the two beds there was a dresser and a table with two chairs. It was pretty Spartan.

She went into the bathroom and was pleased to discover that there were two sinks and plenty of tiny bottles of soaps, shampoos, and lotions. The room itself was also white with an occasional tan accent tile. She knew it was supposed to be soothing, help her clear her mind, but the lack of color just disturbed her somehow.

"I could never attend one of these things for real," she muttered.

"I know, it's odd, isn't it?" Jeremiah asked from the other room.

She shook her head. His super-keen hearing was something he hadn't bothered trying to hide from her since their experiences in Israel. Sometimes she still forgot, though, that when she was talking to herself he could hear her.

"No privacy at all around this place," she whispered, smiling at herself in the mirror.

"We'll know for sure in a minute," Jeremiah said as he walked into the bathroom.

His eyes were sweeping the room and he started checking under the counter, the light fixtures, everything. She knew he was searching for recording devices. She moved back into the bedroom to get out of his way while he was doing that. She picked up the schedule of events from the table where Jeremiah had put it down. She sat down on the edge of her bed as she looked it over.

"The meet and greet starts at 4:30 with dinner at 6:00," she told him. "Those are the only things scheduled for today. Apparently tomorrow morning breakfast is served at 7:30 and at 9:00 we do some kind of group session before breaking at noon for lunch. It looks like at 2:00 we have yoga. There's a small group session at 3:00. We have our first meeting with Dr. Carpenter at 4:00. Then we have dinner at 6:00 followed by another group meeting at 7:30."

"Sounds like they're going to keep us busy," Jeremiah said as he walked into the room.

"It will be interesting to see what we do. I've never been to anything like this before."

"Neither have I."

"I've done one or two religious retreats and my parents made me go to summer camp once, but that's it," she said.

Jeremiah was moving around the bedroom, still on his bug hunt. She kept reading the schedule, hoping she sounded casual. "It says there will be a horseback riding opportunity on Thursday. I think I'm going to be skipping that."

"I wouldn't blame you," Jeremiah said. "You haven't exactly had a lot of fun on those kinds of outings."

She made a face at his back before continuing to read. "Apparently there are nature hikes, yoga classes, and clean eating demonstrations you can participate in."

"From the sounds of the schedule when would we have the time?" he asked.

"There must be some free time scheduled in."

"Which we will be using to find out what happened to Malcolm," he said, turning toward her.

It startled her, his saying the man's name that way. "So, I take it you didn't find anything?" she asked, eyebrows raised.

"No, room's clean. For now, at least."

"Well, that's a relief."

"Anyway, it looks like we have a few hours now before we're expected anywhere. Let's get to work," he said. He picked up the map of the facility from the table, folded it, and put it in his pocket. "The sooner we figure this out, the sooner we can go home."

"Okay, where do we start?"

"First, we walk around, meet as many of the staff as we can without looking suspicious, and I'll take a look at their security, taking special note of cameras, things like that. That way it will be easier when I break into the computers tonight and see what I can find out about Malcolm.

Cindy felt her heart start to race a little. "Won't that be dangerous?"

He gave her a long look. "We're here undercover, aren't we?"

"Yes."

"Okay, so let's play spy."

Her heart was racing even faster now. *Except one of us won't be playing*, she thought.

He held out a hand to her.

She stood, feeling a little breathless, and took it. He laced his fingers through hers and she could feel his warmth, his strength. It seemed to flood through her as though just by holding hands she was sharing in that warmth and strength. She did know that she was feeling insanely happy. Far too happy for someone who was there trying to find a missing man and possibly his killer.

They left their bungalow and strolled slowly back to the main building. They walked for a minute in silence and Cindy found herself looking at everything she could, wondering where security cameras might be lurking. She thought she saw a small red light in one of the bushes near bungalow 10, but she blinked and it seemed to disappear. Maybe she was winding herself up too much.

"Speaking of horseback riding, how is your brother doing?" Jeremiah asked.

"Kyle?" she asked with a frown. Jeremiah usually didn't ask her about her family. He knew the relationships there were complex and could be difficult and frustrating for her. Although after the experience meeting his family, her family dynamic seemed downright normal.

"Do you have another one?" he teased lightly.

"No, he's okay. I mean, I think deep down he's still struggling a little bit with what happened with Lisa. That was a year ago, though, and I think he's finally starting to put it all behind him."

"Oh, what makes you say that?"

"Mom told me he's dating again."

"Does she approve?" Jeremiah asked.

"It's Kyle. You know he can do no wrong in her eyes."

"Work's going well for him, though?"

"Yeah. He's working overtime on the show and apparently the episodes coming up over the summer are going to be legendary, like nothing mortal man has ever dared put on television before," she said, realizing that she couldn't keep the mocking tone out of her voice.

She glanced at Jeremiah and realized that while he had his head tilted slightly toward her, he wasn't looking at her. His eyes were darting around and she realized he was taking everything in, seeing what she didn't. There were times she thought she'd love to spend a day knowing what it was like to be him, to see with his eyes. Then there were days when she knew beyond a shadow of a doubt that she would never want to see the world the way he had to.

When they made it back to the main building they strolled inside still hand-in-hand. It felt so good to be that way, holding hands with him in public, not caring that people saw them. It felt as though a burden was lifting off her and she realized just how stressful hiding their relationship had been for the past several months.

"So, where are you taking me on Valentine's Day?" she asked.

"I haven't decided yet," he said.

She allowed herself a brief fantasy, him in a suit, roses, a candlelight dinner in a nice restaurant, and holding hands on the table, brazen as could be for all the world to see.

Across from the reception desk was the dining room. Next to it were two smaller rooms, one full of gym equipment and the other full of yoga mats. There was a small rack of brochures showcasing the different retreats the center held. Cindy grabbed one of each before they headed out.

They turned to the left, heading down the other row of bungalows. Cindy had the urge to lean her head against Jeremiah's shoulder, but knew that she shouldn't do anything to distract him from what he was doing. Hopefully he was seeing everything he needed to and would be able to figure out how to break into the computer system without getting caught.

When they reached the end of that row of bungalows they found another path and they turned down it. A minute later they arrived at a large building made mostly of glass panes that let the light stream inside. The door was open and they walked in. The room reminded Cindy of their bungalow, white floor and walls with large, tan pillows arranged on the floor.

"I think this might be where we have the large meetings," she commented.

"So, they're going to have us sit on the pillows and spend time gazing into each other's eyes?" he asked.

"I don't know, I guess. Like I said, I've never done anything like this before."

"Well, it will be easy for me. After all, you have such pretty eyes," he said.

She felt herself flush and she smiled up at him. He still wasn't looking at her, instead turning his head slowly so that he took in the entire room. She knew he needed to, but she still felt a twinge of disappointment. She could have gone for some eye gazing right then.

"They say the eyes are the windows to the soul," she said softly.

"They are what they need to be," he responded cryptically.

"Hello, may I help you?"

Cindy turned to see a man walking into the room. He was dressed from head to toe in loose, white clothing. He had long, straight dark hair and green eyes that stared at her intently.

"We're just touring the grounds. We're here for the couples' retreat," she said with a smile.

"Welcome. I'm Arnold, I'll be one of your guides on your journey," he said, walking forward with hand extended.

"Jeremiah and Cindy," Jeremiah said as they each shook the man's hand.

"It's a pleasure to welcome you here to our little oasis of serenity," the man said with a slightly syrupy grin. Cindy didn't like him and she struggled to keep the smile on her face.

"We're just thrilled to be here," she said.

"So, what brings the two of you here?"

Jeremiah took a deep breath. "Well, we're here to, I guess, decide what the future has in store."

"Ah, you're at a crossroads in your relationship," Arnold said knowingly.

"You could say that," Jeremiah answered, his tone a bit cool.

Cindy glanced up at him. Jeremiah was smiling, but it was a cold smile that didn't light up his face like his genuine ones did.

"Well, I can assure you that there is no better place to get away, relax, reflect, and find your way than here. My staff and I will do everything in our power to make your journey as fulfilling as possible."

"Your staff? Are you the manager?" Cindy asked.

"The owner, actually, but I prefer to think of us as one big, happy family."

Even the way he said that made her feel slightly uncomfortable. His words were smooth, oily almost, and they seemed to slide over her as though he was seeking to lull her into a false sense of security. The word that bubbled up in her mind was *snake*.

But she forced herself to smile at the serpent that was smiling at her. She couldn't help but think that they might have already found the person responsible for Malcolm's disappearance. It took every ounce of willpower she had to not let her true feelings show.

She felt Jeremiah's fingers tighten slightly around hers. She wondered if he was sensing her desire to get away from Arnold.

"You have a beautiful facility, it must have cost a fortune to build," Jeremiah said.

Jeremiah was trying to get something out of the man. Talking about the cost of things was something he wasn't prone to doing otherwise.

"A little, but I was raised to believe that if you're going to do something, you have to do it to the best of your ability, give it everything you have. That's the only way to go through life. Wouldn't you agree?"

"Of course."

"And the cost was worth it. Every day I am repaid a thousand times over when a client tells us that we have helped them in some way."

He was lying. She felt it instinctively. The money was important to him, but she had a feeling the one thing that meant even more than that was image. And he was doing his best to sell an image to them. Only she wasn't buying and she was sure Jeremiah wasn't either.

"Could you tell us a little more about the group sessions?" Cindy asked. Jeremiah wasn't ending the conversation so he must be still acquiring information. The least she could do was help stall until he was ready to leave.

"Actually, I'd prefer to wait until a little later this afternoon when I'll be able to talk to everyone at once."

"We understand," Jeremiah said.

"I appreciate that. Now, if you'll excuse me, I have a few things still to prepare before the meet-and-greet."

"Of course, we'll just continue our little tour," Jeremiah said.

They turned and they left the glass building. As they did so, the hair on the back of Cindy's neck suddenly lifted and she felt a chill dance down her spine. She turned her head and saw Arnold standing in the middle of the room, a smile on his face, but there was a shadow in his eyes.

6

Jeremiah could tell that Cindy was ready to declare Arnold responsible for what happened to Malcolm. He wasn't convinced yet, but the man did have a sliminess about him that made Jeremiah uncomfortable. They continued walking and soon came upon a couple of smaller rooms that were set up like the glass one only with far fewer cushions on the floor. He guessed these were the smaller group meeting rooms.

As they walked they also discovered a large pool with sand surrounding it to imitate a beach, a restroom area, a small covered hut set up with two massage tables, and three buildings that were marked with Staff Only signs. Throughout it all he only saw three security cameras. A resort hotel would have had more than that. He couldn't decide if the lack of them here was to protect the privacy of the clientele or the staff. Either way it was good for him as far as being able to have pretty free range of the place. It was bad if they were looking for any video evidence of what might have happened to Malcolm.

For a place that was about to be host to a weeklong retreat there didn't seem to be that many staff about. It was possible they were in meetings or weren't scheduled to go on shift until closer to the meet-and-greet. He didn't see any guests walking around either. It was possible he and Cindy were the first to arrive. If there were other guests they must be staying in their rooms.

"It's pretty here, but kind of weird feeling," Cindy finally remarked.

"That's because it's starting to feel like we're the only two people here," he said.

"That's true. All we've seen is the woman at the front desk and Arnold. I guess I'm not used to being out of the house and not surrounded by people."

"One of the hazards of living in a large metropolitan area," he mused. "Still, this place does feel like it's hibernating."

"That's it, that's exactly what it feels like. It's not like it's completely devoid of life, it's more like what is here just isn't showing itself."

She shivered suddenly. He let go of her hand and instead put an arm around her shoulders, pulling her close. After a moment she put her arm around his waist and leaned her head against him as they walked.

"You changed your shampoo," he noted. "It smells like strawberries."

"Do you like it?" she asked.

"I do."

He liked it a little too much. He realized all his attention was beginning to shift to her. They had almost walked the entire grounds, though, and he had seen what he needed to. He let his mind drift for just a moment, thinking about her.

He knew she wasn't happy with the current state of things between them. He knew the secrecy was bothering her, but he was trying to protect them both. He wasn't sure she realized that going public with their relationship would most likely bring a firestorm down on both of them. Sometimes he hated being the one that had to worry about that. There were days he wished he could throw caution to the wind entirely. That wasn't in his nature, though. In his line of work you always had to have a plan and a backup plan, and a backup to your backup if you wanted to survive.

He took a deep breath, reminding himself that the need for those plans was related to his former line of work, not his current one. He was a rabbi. He still had to think things through because other people relied on him, looked up to him, but his decisions were no longer a matter of life and death.

"What are you thinking?" Cindy asked.

He kissed the top of her head. "I really like the shampoo."

Having encountered no other staff members to question, they finally headed back to their bungalow. As they passed bungalow number five he heard raised voices, a man and a woman arguing about something although he wasn't quite sure what.

After they had passed by Cindy said, "I guess some couples are going to need more help than others. At least we know we won't be the only ones here."

"Yes, that would have been awkward."

Once they were back in their bungalow Jeremiah did a second sweep for any listening devices. Then he settled down at the table with the map of the resort and began studying it.

Cindy went to work unpacking, putting her things away in the closet and the dresser. Out of the corner of his eye he saw her hang up a red dress that didn't look familiar. He realized that, like her current outfit, it must be new. From what he had glimpsed of the dress it didn't look like Cindy's style. She usually dressed pretty conservatively.

He couldn't help but wonder if Geanie and she had gone shopping together. Even as he continued to study the map he found himself imagining how Cindy would look in the dress. With a sigh he forced himself to refocus. They had only a couple hours left before the retreat began and he wanted to be as prepared as he could be.

Mark felt like he was being torn in two. He hated that he'd left Cindy and Jeremiah behind, even if he knew Jeremiah could almost certainly handle whatever was thrown at them. He had decided to investigate Malcolm on his end and see what he could find out about the man including whether he had any enemies and whether there was anything suspicious in his financial records.

Even as he tried to focus, though, his thoughts kept getting pulled back to Not Paul and the strange fact that the attorney he had entrusted things to was now dead. Even though he had finally learned Paul's true identity he had never felt like he could close the case on the mystery that was his old partner. The other attorney, Fred Mitchell, was supposed to call him back tomorrow with what he'd found in the man's files about Paul.

That was assuming that Paul hadn't used an alias when dealing with the attorney.

That was also assuming that Fred wasn't busy destroying evidence right at that moment.

You're being paranoid, he told himself. It didn't make him feel any better. The way things had been running for him the last couple of years his paranoid thoughts had been turning out to be not so paranoid. That in itself could certainly make a man twice as paranoid.

Pull it together.

The problem was, the law firm in northern California was a seven hour drive away. It wasn't like he could just show up there on a whim. This wasn't even an active investigation. If he did that, he'd be doing it on his own time, and leaving his friends and family in the lurch.

There was something, though, something pulling at his insides, that wouldn't let him drop it. With a sigh he put on his bluetooth and turned his car around. He called Liam and a few seconds later his partner picked up.

"Hey, how did the trial go?"

"Good. I don't see how the jury could come back with anything other than a guilty verdict," Liam said.

Mark grimaced. "Yeah, and yet sometimes they surprise you and come back with a verdict that makes absolutely no sense. Those are the times I'd pay money just to be in there watching everything fall apart."

"I think it would be too hard to watch and not intervene," Liam said. "At any rate, my part of it is over finally. No more testimony required."

"That's good, just in time."

"In time for what?" Liam asked, sounding justifiably suspicious.

"To cover for me."

"With whom?"

"With everyone. I need to take a quick trip up north to check on a couple of things."

"What things?"

"Leads."

There was such a long pause that Mark thought that the call might have dropped. Finally Liam asked, "Does this have something to do with Paul?"

Mark weighed his answer carefully. Liam was a good man, a good cop, and he trusted him with his life. Liam was the only one who'd been willing to work with him after Mark had tortured that one suspect. Liam was kind, forgiving, and easy to get along with. He also walked the straight and narrow more than anyone else on the force. Although Liam had proven that he was willing to adapt to some unconventional police methods, Mark wasn't sure how he'd respond if he knew the truth.

Still, Liam was his partner and Mark owed him that much. After all, it's what he wished Paul had given to him.

"Yes, it does. There's been a new development and I need to run it down before evidence is destroyed."

He was only stretching the truth a little bit. After all, the whole reason he wanted to drive up there was to make sure it wasn't being destroyed.

There was another pause before Liam said, "Good luck, Mark. Let me know if there's anything you need from me."

"Thanks, Liam, if I need you or your arsenal I'll be sure to let you know."

As soon as Mark hung up with Liam he called Traci. He briefly told her where he was headed.

When he had finished she said, "You haven't really thought this through, have you?"

"No, why?"

"By the time you get there tonight the office will be closed. You don't have any kind of a search warrant or legitimate police backing so it's not like you can just go in and find what you want. You're going to have to find someplace to stay the night and then go the office first thing in the morning."

He paused as he felt frustration sinking in. "You're right."

"Of course I am."

"If you take a plane you can make it before the end of the business day and be back tonight. In the long run that will be cheaper than a hotel, several meals, and the gas you'll use."

"You're a genius."

"I know. I'm also a very tired mom who wants you on diaper duty tonight."

"Yes, ma'am," he said as he changed freeways to head for the airport.

Cindy was in the bathroom of the bungalow she was sharing with Jeremiah, staring at herself in the mirror. She looked good, great even. She was surprised to admit it. She was wearing the black dress that Wildman had helped pick out. She was worried that she might be a little overdressed for the meet-and-greet. This was the most conservative of the dresses she had brought with her, though. She was beginning to wonder if it had been a mistake to let Wildman talk her into it.

She had done her hair up because it felt more appropriate to wear her hair that way with a dress like this. She was wearing more makeup than just her usual lipstick. She had on blush and had even gone as far as eyeshadow and mascara.

"Are you almost ready?" Jeremiah called.

"Yes," she said. She gave herself a smile, turned, and exited the bathroom.

Jeremiah was standing up from the table and he froze partway up. His eyes widened and quickly swept her from head to toe.

"How do I look?" she asked as she did a quick turn.

"Stunning," he said, his voice sounding a little deeper. He finished standing up and quickly walked over to her, a smile spreading across his features.

"Absolutely stunning."

"Thank you. You look very handsome."

He was wearing a black button down shirt and a pair of khaki colored slacks.

"I wish you'd told me we were dressing up. I would have packed a suit."

"I think you look perfect the way you are. Besides, it's perfectly acceptable if the woman dresses more upscale than the man but not the other way around."

"Oh really?" he asked, lifting an eyebrow.

"So I've been told." She glanced over at the table and the papers he had spread across it. "Did you find anything?"

"Not yet. I'm making sure I've memorized the area, just in case."

"Sounds like a good idea. I probably should, too," she said.

"We can talk about that after dinner. Shall we?"

"Yes."

They exited the bungalow and then Jeremiah offered her his arm. She took it and as they walked she couldn't help but feel like this whole twisted thing was a real date.

They walked toward the glass building and Cindy suddenly realized that her choice of attire might have been a bad one after all. She tried to imagine how she was going to get up and down off one of the cushions on the floor without flashing everyone let alone maintaining some semblance of dignity and grace.

When they reached the building she saw to her relief that the pillows had been stacked up along the one wall, clearing the floor. Apparently the meet-and-greet would be more like a mixer where everyone stood and milled around.

A table had been set up along one wall with glasses of champagne on it. The man they had met earlier, Arnold, was standing near it wearing casual slacks, a white shirt with the top button undone and a sports jacket. He was chatting to an older couple. The man was wearing a suit and the woman was wearing a dress and some very expensive looking pearls. The couple didn't strike Cindy as the type to go in for a retreat like this.

Two other couples were already there as well. They were standing together. Or, rather, the men were standing together and the women were standing a couple feet away, intent on something.

She and Jeremiah walked over. As soon as they got close all four looked up at them and then moved quickly forward with greetings.

"Hi, we're the Werthers, Kim and Levi," the shorter man with brown hair said, holding out his hand.

"Cindy and Jeremiah," Jeremiah said, introducing them.

"Hi," Kim, a redhead with brilliant green eyes, said.

They shook hands with both of them. Then the second couple who were both tall, blond, and tan introduced themselves.

"We're Jack and Jill," the man said. "I know, but it's true. And believe it or not I did not marry her for her name," he said.

"But I married him for his," Jill said quickly.

They both threw back their heads and laughed.

Almost like a pair of hyenas, Cindy couldn't help but think. She was about to chide herself for being unkind, but they kept going for what seemed like forever. When they finally stopped laughing it was unnaturally abrupt, almost like they had decided that was the moment to stop.

"Have you seen who's with us?" Jill asked, without skipping a beat. She pointed to the couple standing next to Arnold.

"Do you know them?" Cindy asked.

Jack and Jill both laughed again. This time, mercifully, it was shorter than the last. As before, though, they stopped abruptly. Without even taking a breath Jill said, "Only in my wildest fantasies! That's Dorothea and Flynn Castleback."

"They're millionaires," Kim said.

"Billionaires," Jill corrected.

Jim laughed and clapped a hand on Jeremiah's shoulder. "I bet yours is just as into society and fashion and all that as ours are."

Before Cindy or Jeremiah could say a word, Jill and Kim had each taken one of Cindy's arms. "Ignore them, Cindy," Kim said as they pulled her a few feet away. "Now we were just trying to figure out, how long exactly do you think that strand of pearls is?"

"I wouldn't know," Cindy said, glancing at Dorothea Castleback.

"I say it's one really long strand looped three times," Kim said.

"And I say that's three separate strands," Jill said.

"They're very pretty," Cindy said, having nothing constructive to add to their debate.

"Gorgeous. You can tell from here how expensive they are," Jill said. "I tell you, if Jack ever bought me a necklace that fine I would never bring it to a place like this in a million years. I would leave it in the safe at home. You know how it is with vacations. It seems like something always gets... lost."

And by "lost" she clearly meant stolen.

Two more couples arrived in the room and eventually Jill and Kim had seized the opportunity to tell them all about Dorothea's pearls as well.

Fortunately within a few minutes the place had filled up. It looked like there were couples from all age ranges present. It might be interesting to hear some of their stories. There were also a few individuals that she suspected were staff at the resort.

After a couple more minutes Arnold clapped his hands together three times. Apparently it was the magic signal for silence because everyone suddenly became quiet. The man wasn't smiling as he looked out over those assembled. She still didn't like him and with the look on his face now she liked him less.

Jeremiah walked up behind her and put a hand on her shoulder, squeezing it gently. She took a deep breath. His touch always reassured her and helped her calm down.

Here we go, she thought to herself.

"Ladies and gentlemen, so glad you could make it. I am Arnold Smith. I have some announcements to make, but first it is imperative that I tell you something and that you hear me, really hear me."

He paused and looked around the room, meeting everyone's eyes.

"All of you are in terrible, terrible danger."

7

There was a ripple effect throughout the room as people shifted uncomfortably but remained silent. Jeremiah squeezed Cindy's shoulder harder, and she could feel his muscles tensing. She couldn't see him but she imagined his eyes were already flitting around the room, seeking out any threats.

"You heard me, right," Arnold said gravely. "You are all in terrible danger of having stale, unfulfilling, monotonous relationships. The divorce statistics in this country are appalling and many of those who decide to stick with their marriage still find themselves feeling trapped, unloved, and unappreciated. The good news is, you've taken the first step toward escaping this danger. You're here which means you're ready and willing to work on gaining a deeper appreciation of your significant other and making the relationship a fulfilling one for you both. The staff here is dedicated to helping you."

He paused and then he smiled. "Tomorrow we're going to be plunging right into it and it will be fun, but it will be hard work as well. Tonight, though, we celebrate. Everyone, grab a glass of champagne and prepare to join me in a toast."

People nearest the table began grabbing and passing glasses until everyone had one.

"Ladies and gentlemen," Arnold said, his glass raised high. "I celebrate your relationships and look forward to helping you build ones that will last a lifetime. Cheers!"

"Cheers," Cindy muttered as she clinked glasses with Jeremiah. She hesitated for a moment and then took a small sip of the champagne. Even though her mind had gone there, she seriously doubted that someone would have poisoned the champagne.

It wasn't like Malcolm's entire retreat group had gone missing, just him. It had probably been something very personal to him and not something sinister involving the entire retreat center.

She noticed that Jeremiah barely sipped his as well. She turned her attention back to Arnold.

"Okay, now that the serious portion of the evening is over, welcome to the retreat!" Arnold said.

A few people cheered, most clapped.

"We are going to have a seriously great time getting intense and personal. This is a safe place. Emotions might run high, but that's okay. Sometimes you might hate me, you might even hate your spouse, but I guarantee that when you leave here it will be with a newfound appreciation for them."

Around the room heads were bobbing up and down.

"For some of you this may be your first time doing something like this, that's okay, we'll hold your hand through the entire process. Others might have been to a couples' retreat somewhere else before. I'd encourage you to just empty your mind of any preconceived notions you might have. I can assure you that we are unlike anything you've experienced before. We delve deeper and play harder here than anywhere else."

More head bobbing around the room. She noticed that while most people were smiling there were a few that looked a bit skeptical.

All of the staff had grins plastered on their faces. They were all huge and seemingly so identical that it was a little creepy. Clearly their instructions for the evening consisted of "smile like your life, or at least your job, depends on it."

"Alright everyone, go ahead, mingle, get to know the other couples and the staff. You're going to be working closely with all these people for the next week. In about half an hour we'll head over to the dining room for dinner."

Around them couples started introducing themselves to one another while Jeremiah and Cindy made a beeline for some of the staffers ringing the room. The first one they reached was a young woman with long brown hair that fell to her waist. She was very petite overall.

"Hi, I'm Cindy and this is Jeremiah," Cindy said, extending her hand to the woman.

"I'm Summer. I'm the yoga instructor. You must be our dating couple, is that right?"

"Yes," Cindy said.

"I have to say it is highly unusual to see a dating couple here. We've had a couple of engaged couples that were just trying to get in pre-nuptial bonding, but I don't think we've ever seen a dating couple before," Summer said as she shook hands with both of them.

"We...have some issues we'd like to work through," Cindy said, suddenly regretting that she hadn't let them just pretend to be a married couple. By being the only dating couple to ever attend the retreat they were sticking out like a sore thumb instead of blending into the background.

There was nothing that could be done about that now, though.

"Well, this is a great place to do that," Summer said. "I wish you both the best of luck."

"Thank you," Jeremiah said.

They moved down the line and introduced themselves to a tall, well-muscled man named Dimitri who turned out to have a thick Russian accent.

"And what do you do here, Dimitri?" Jeremiah asked.

"I am the ballroom dance instructor," he said.

"Excuse me?" Cindy asked, sure she couldn't have heard him right.

"I teach dance, the ultimate physical expression of intimacy and partnership between a man and a woman."

"Oh, okay," she said, feeling a bit flustered. Jeremiah was a much better dancer than she was and she always felt a bit nervous at the thought of dancing.

She hastily moved on to a short man with glasses and thinning hair. "Hi, Cindy," she said, holding out her hand.

"Dr. Carpenter, staff psychologist," he said.

His hand was limp in hers as she shook it which unnerved her more than the intensity of the ballroom dance instructor. He turned beady eyes toward Jeremiah. "And you must be the boyfriend," he said, and the way he said it made it sound very unflattering.

"Yes, I am," Jeremiah said, a little aggression coming out in his voice.

Dr. Carpenter did not extend his hand to Jeremiah, instead he deliberately put his hand in his pocket.

Cindy was shocked at the display of rudeness. Dr. Carpenter didn't know Jeremiah, they'd only just met. There was no need to be condescending and rude toward him. Plus, wasn't the guy's job to help all the couples deepen their relationships and smile while doing so? He couldn't possibly be this way with everyone, could he?

Jeremiah put his hand on her waist and gently pushed, signaling that they should move on. She did and they presented themselves to the next staff member, a woman with dusky skin, dancing eyes and a brilliant smile.

"I'm Jasmine," she said brightly.

"Jeremiah and Cindy," Jeremiah said, stretching out his hand.

She rolled her eyes. "Please, I'm a hugger," she said, stepping forward and hugging first him then Cindy. "Trust me, by the time I'm through with you, you'll both be huggers, too," she said.

"What do you do here?" Cindy asked when Jasmine had finally let go of her.

"I mostly run some of the small group sessions," she said. "We focus a lot on communication and intimacy. Or, as my girl Ursula said, 'the importance of body language'."

Cindy couldn't help but laugh out loud when she realized Jasmine was quoting from the Disney movie, *The Little Mermaid.*

"See, you know what I'm talking about," Jasmine said with a mischievous glint in her eye.

Cindy could have stood and talked with the other woman all night. She had a way of putting someone at ease even if she was a hugger. She kept in mind, though, that they needed to meet as many of the staff as they could to aid in their investigation.

"I look forward to talking with you later," Cindy said before they moved on.

"I really hope she doesn't have anything to do with it," Cindy whispered to Jeremiah.

"I would be genuinely surprised if she did," he replied.

They met five others before Arnold announced that it was time to head to dinner.

In the dining room they discovered that there were three couples assigned to each table.

Cindy was pleased to see that they were at a table near the door which was perfect if they needed to make a hasty exit. She was less thrilled to see that Jack and Jill were at their table. She had been a bit put off by Jill and Kim when talking with them earlier. The other couple at their table she hadn't met yet.

"Isn't this fabulous?" Jill said in a giggly voice as they all prepared to sit down. "It would only be better if Kim were here, too."

Cindy glanced around the room. Kim and Levi were sitting down across the room by a large picture window. Cindy noticed that they were at Dorothea and Flynn's table and that Kim had wasted no time in trying to get her hands on the older woman's pearls. Kim was leaning in and touching them as though examining the strand.

"Looks like she's sitting at Dorothea's table," Cindy said.

Jill spun quickly, eyes zeroing in on Kim and Dorothea.

"Why that little-" Jill started to mumble under her breath before she grabbed a passing staff member by the arm. "Excuse me, I really need to be moved to that table over by the window."

"I'm sorry, ma'am, all the seating arrangements have been finalized," the man said.

"But you don't understand, I have to sit over there," Jill wailed.

"Ma'am, I assure you every table is an excellent one."

Cindy could swear she could actually see the gears in Jill's mind turning. She was clearly not going to let Kim get the upper hand when it came to schmoozing the rich, older couple. She glanced at Jack to see what he thought of his wife's behavior. He stood beside his chair, just watching the exchange, face passive.

"It's not good enough!" Jill said, her voice raising and drawing the attention of more people.

"What seems to be the problem?" Arnold asked, suddenly appearing.

"I'm, I'm claustrophobic. I simply must sit by the window where I can see outside," Jill said. "That table," she added, pointing.

Cindy gaped at her. It was such an obvious bald-faced lie. The others had to see through it.

"Come with me and we will see what we can do," Arnold said.

With a smug grin Jill set out after him, and Jack followed behind. Cindy watched as they reached the other side of the room. Arnold said something quietly to the people at that table. After a moment Dorothea and Flynn rose, much to Jill's obvious chagrin.

A few moments later the older couple were seating themselves at Cindy and Jeremiah's table.

"I'm sorry they made you move," Cindy said.

"We volunteered," Flynn said. "It seemed like a good excuse to move."

"I don't know what was wrong with that one girl. She kept touching my throat. I thought she was going to attempt to strangle me," Dorothea said.

Cindy bit her lip to keep from laughing out loud. Once she had managed to restrain herself she said, "I know she and the girl you swapped seats with were admiring your pearl necklace earlier. I imagine she was just trying to get a closer look."

"Any closer and I would have been wearing *her* around my neck instead of the pearls," Dorothea said drily.

"That's an image I'd rather not see," Jeremiah said.

"Me either," Flynn chimed in.

They made introductions around the table. The third couple were Beth and Tristan from Nevada. They seemed nice, but they were both very quiet. They had been married for ten years. Dorothea and Flynn had been married for thirty-six years.

Cindy glanced over to the table by the window and saw that both Jill and Kim were staring over at them. She had a sudden, insane urge to give them a little wave, but she restrained herself. It wasn't a good idea to antagonize anyone here, particularly since they didn't want to draw attention to themselves.

"You doing okay?" Jeremiah asked.

"Yes," she said, turning to him with a smile.

As dinner dragged on Cindy found herself with more and more butterflies in her stomach. It was as though with every passing moment the reality of the fact that they were here as spies to ferret out the truth came home a little bit more. The anxiety must have started showing on her face because suddenly Jeremiah was rubbing her shoulders.

"You need to relax, there's no need to worry about work or anything else right now," he said. He looked at the others. "My Cindy is a bit of a perfectionist, and she sometime has a hard time letting go."

Around the table heads bobbed up and down in understanding.

"I'm sorry, it's been a busy few weeks and I'm afraid it will take me a little while to unwind and put it all behind me," she said.

"You will, though, dear," Dorothea said sympathetically. "This is the place to do it as well. The staff here are always so courteous and friendly they make it easy."

"You've been here before?" Cindy asked.

"Many times," Flynn said with a smile for his wife. "We've found it very helpful to come once a year and really get in touch with each other, reconnect."

"So you're here every year?" Jeremiah asked.

"Yes, just like clockwork. We come to celebrate our anniversary. We used to take trips, but we realized that we were engaging in activities that were focusing us outward instead of inward on us and our relationship," Dorothea said.

"Well, it must be working. You two seem to be going strong," Beth said, her voice almost a little wistful.

"It's done wonders for our marriage. You'll see, it can help yours, too," Flynn said.

"That's why we're here," Tristan said.

Dorothea and Flynn both turned to look at Cindy and Jeremiah. Cindy was a little taken aback by the intensity of their stares.

82

"And it will help you, too. If you survive it," Dorothea said bluntly.

"What do you mean, 'survive it'?" Cindy asked.

"Don't let tonight fool you. They might be all love and flowers tonight, but the staff are relentless. If you have weaknesses in your relationship they will find them and force you to deal with them. It won't be pretty or pleasant by any stretch of the imagination," Flynn said.

"It's hardest on those who aren't married yet. For the rest of us we keep at it and work at it because no one who comes here wants a divorce and we all know how nasty and protracted those can become. For the engaged couples that come here, though, it's different because they can just get up and walk away without the same ramifications and legal repercussions. They come in all lovey dovey, you know, pawing at each other and everything, but when things get real they can't handle it. Marriage is hard work and so many people don't understand that ahead of time," Dorothea said.

"Surely some of the engaged couples make it," Cindy said. "I mean, they must want to work through their differences if they've come to a place like this."

Flynn shook his head. "They come expecting to get couples' massages while being told how perfect they are for each other. Either that or they come expecting to change something about the other person. Either way they end up disappointed and then angry."

"Do you know that in all the years we've been coming to this place not once have we seen an engaged couple get through the week together?" Dorothea said. "It's always very sad."

"Then it's a good thing we're just dating," Jeremiah said, clearly trying to lighten the mood.

Cindy was again kicking herself for not having gone along with the fake marriage story. She'd had no idea just how much attention they would get because they weren't married.

"You seem like a nice young couple. I'm sure you'll be fine," Flynn said, with a half-smile.

He didn't mean it, though. Cindy could tell, and it upset her. She told herself that there was no reason to get upset, but she couldn't fight it. Jeremiah didn't say anything, but he kept massaging her shoulders.

Mark was cursing the fact that he'd opted to rent a car for the evening instead of just taking a cab to the law firm. By the time he pulled into the parking lot it was six o'clock and he was worried he might have missed everyone. It really depended on what type of law firm it was. Some had its employees working insanely late into the night. Others adhered to rigid business hours.

He parked the car and walked quickly toward the front of the building. There were still a good number of cars in the parking lot so he might be able to catch someone in. Part of him still felt like he was on a fool's errand. If his worst fears were true and the firm was destroying evidence about Paul, they would have likely done so right after he called the other day.

Just keep it together and act like this is a normal case, he told himself. *Even if someone is in, it'll probably be one of the most boring evenings of your life.*

As Mark reached the front door of the building it burst open and two security guards half-dragged, half-carried a kicking, screaming woman outside.

8

Mark quickly got over his shock and moved toward them, flashing his badge. "Police officer, what's going on here?"

He had no jurisdiction whatsoever, but he was relying on them not actually paying close enough attention to realize that until he got a couple of answers.

The front door swung open and another woman emerged, this one carrying a file box. She spoke up, clearly having heard Mark's question. "Ms. Alvarez has been fired. Didn't want to leave calmly, so we're escorting her to her car."

"Twelve years and this is all the thanks I get?" the woman shouted. "I worked just as hard to build this firm up as anyone else!"

"Ms. Alvarez, are you going to go quietly or do we need to involve the police?" the woman with the file box asked, voice menacing.

Mark definitely felt like he had stepped right in the middle of something. Before he could say anything, though, the woman who seemed to be in charge put the box down and turned to him.

"Is there something I can help you with?"

"I'm here to see Mr. Mitchell."

"You don't have an appointment," she said matter-of-factly.

"No, but it is a police matter," he said, fudging the truth and hoping he didn't get caught.

"We are always happy to cooperate with the police," she said. "Let me escort you inside." She glared at the security guards. "And you two, escort Ms. Alvarez to her car."

She turned and opened the door, sashaying inside, and leaving Mark to catch the door as he followed behind. She was in complete control and she knew it, her entire manner was arrogant, condescending. She moved to the elevator bank and waited, tapping her toe impatiently.

The doors slid open and she marched inside and punched a button. The doors started to close on Mark as he squeezed his way in. She pressed a manicured nail against the button for the fourth floor. Then drummed her fingernails against the elevator wall as it began its slow ascent.

She was trying to unsettle him. What was frustrating was that it was working. Several seconds later the doors finally opened and she exited with Mark right on her heels. After a couple of quick turns they arrived at Fred Mitchell's office.

The man was standing, coat over his arm, turning off his computer.

"Excuse me, sir, there is a police officer here to see you," the woman said.

The attorney frowned slightly as he turned toward them. "I wasn't expecting anyone."

"No, sorry for the drop-in," Mark said, stepping forward.

"That's fine. Thank you, Nina. You can go home, I'll see you in the morning."

The woman nodded, turned and left without a word to Mark. Fred, meanwhile, slung his jacket over the back of his chair, sat down, and leaned his elbows on his desk.

"Your voice sounds familiar."

"That's because we spoke on the phone the other day. I'm Detective Mark Walters."

"Oh, that's right, yes. I believe I was going to call you tomorrow?"

"Yes, but I was...in the area and decided there was no time like the present."

"Fine, I understand. I'm just sorry you took the time when I don't have better news for you."

"Oh?"

"Yes, I'm afraid we've searched the files for the entire firm and we haven't found any references to a Paul Dryer. I even sent someone over to the facility that stores our archive of cases that were closed more than ten years ago, but they called a few minutes ago to let me know they'd struck out. I'm sorry."

"And did you search Kent Gordon's personal files?"

Fred shook his head. "He didn't have any. None of our staff do. That's corporate policy. At the end of the business days all files and notes are checked back in to our filing room which is the most secure spot in the building. Then they're checked out again in the morning if they're needed. Kent was killed in a car accident on his way to work. Everything he'd been working on the day before was in the file room. I personally cleaned out his desk and gave his things to his wife. There was nothing but office supplies and personal mementos."

"And I'm assuming that his office has been put back into use?"

"Yes, we promoted one of our newer associates and he got the office after Kent's things were cleared out. I'm sorry, but it looks like you've hit a dead end."

He was lying, Mark was sure of it. He just didn't know what about. It could be that he was being honest about not finding any mention of Paul, but lying about the fact that Kent had files in his office.

One thing was clear. He wasn't going to get anything out of the man.

"Thank you for looking," Mark said.

"It was no problem. We are always happy to cooperate with the police."

Mark felt a sudden chill. That was exactly what Nina had said, word for word. It was a practiced answer.

Mark turned to go, then paused and turned back deliberately. "If you have AAA you might want to be calling them soon. I saw a Ms. Alvarez being escorted from the building earlier and I wouldn't put it past her to slash someone's tires. She had that look to her."

"Melinda?" Fred said with a frown. "She does have a temper. I just hope you're not right. I've got a dinner engagement I can't afford to be late for."

Mark shrugged. "Hopefully I'm wrong. Thanks again for your help."

Mark turned and headed out of the office and then made his way downstairs. He knew one person he needed to talk to. He was pretty sure there was no way he'd pry Melinda's home address out of anyone here, though.

As soon as he made it to the car he searched for a Melinda Alvarez on social media sites. When he had found her it he was able to get her date of birth as well. He called Liam, asking him to do a DMV search for her.

A few minutes later Liam called back with her address. Mark punched it into the GPS unit that had come with the car and determined that she was only about twenty minutes away.

As he headed out of the parking lot he just hoped that she'd gone straight home instead of somewhere to drown her sorrows. He had a feeling she had information he needed and that her firing today was not a coincidence.

Traffic was a mess and with all the delays it took him twice as long as it should have to reach her house. When he finally got there he parked on the street in front and quickly walked up to ring the bell.

There was no response and after a minute he rang it again and followed up with a knock on the door.

He was just about to give up when he heard locks being turned. The door opened and Melinda Alvarez stared at him.

"I left, what more do they want from me?" she asked.

He shook his head. "I'm not in any way connected with your former employer. I do, however, need your help. I've been investigating a case for a while now and I have a feeling that there's something Fred Mitchell is hiding from me."

"That's something you'll have to take up with him. I don't work there anymore," she said.

"Why did they fire you?" he pressed.

She hesitated and then seemed to give in. "I objected to some bad business practices. I caught them destroying files this afternoon. First they tried to pass it off as nothing, shredding unnecessary documentation that had already been archived offsite. It didn't smell right to me, though, so I pushed and then they pushed back."

Mark could feel his excitement level rising. "Do you know whose files they were shredding?"

"No, I don't."

"Have you ever heard the name Paul Dryer?" Mark asked.

The startled look in her eyes was confirmation that she had.

"Please," Mark said. "It's urgent that I get some answers about him."

She nodded slowly and then stepped back so he could walk inside. After closing the door she led him to a kitchen table.

"Would you like some water?" she asked.

"No, thank you."

She nodded and grabbed a bottle for herself out of the refrigerator before joining him at the table.

"How do you know Paul Dryer?" she asked.

"We worked together for several years at the Pine Springs Police Department. He was my partner. How do you know him?"

"He was one of Kent's clients."

"So, when Fred told me they couldn't find any files mentioning him, he was lying?"

She frowned. "Maybe. Maybe not. Like I said, I don't know what files they were destroying earlier. What I do know is that Kent represented Paul Dryer privately. He was Kent's client before Kent began working for the firm. When things like that happen then normally either the attorney-client relationship is terminated or the client becomes the client of the firm."

"Normally?"

"Yes. Look, I started off just working for Kent when he was a solo practitioner. When the firm hired him he insisted that they hire me, too. Since his death I've been a floater, working for whichever attorney has the most pressing caseload at that moment. I did that some before his death, too. I mean, we'd all pitch in where needed."

"So, did he take his clients with him to the firm as well?" Mark asked.

"About half of them. The other half just weren't comfortable working with a large firm. He understood that and they parted ways amicably. I handled a lot of the correspondence and a lot of the transferring of paperwork."

"And Paul?"

She took a deep breath. "Paul was his first client. In fact, Kent let it slip once that Paul put him through law school and set him up in business."

"Why?"

"I got the impression it was because Paul wanted or needed an attorney who was beholden to him for some reason."

"You said you handled all the transition paperwork?"

"Yes, but nothing for Paul. That's why I can't be sure if the law firm had any documentation on him. Whatever Kent did he handled it himself. I do suspect, however, that he might have kept him on as a private client on the side."

"What makes you think so?"

"Because every year on November 15th they had a standing meeting. It was automatically put on the calendar as an annual recurring event regardless of the day of the week. This past year was the first time it wasn't on the calendar."

Georgia had said the attorney showed up about eight months after Paul's death because of a missed meeting and that would put it pretty much right as far as timing went.

"If he had kept him on as a private client, where would he have kept Paul's files?" Mark asked.

"At home, in his office," she said.

"And where would that stuff have ended up after Kent died?"

"They would still be there. His wife really hasn't touched any of this things, particularly in that room."

He felt a ray of hope shoot through him. "How can I get in touch with her?"

"You can't right now. She's out of town visiting relatives and won't be home for a couple more weeks."

And just like that he felt deflated again.

Melinda gazed at him shrewdly. "It's important that you see these files right away?"

"It is," he said, forcing himself to take a deep breath.

"Well, then there might be another way."

"What? How?"

She smirked. "I have a key."

"Then what are we waiting for?" Mark asked, standing up.

Twenty minutes later they were pulling into the driveway of a house large enough to be called a small mansion. Mark had let Melinda drive. She parked the car and they both got out and headed for the front door.

"He always had me running back and forth picking up things for him," Melinda said as she unlocked the door and let them inside. She swiftly disarmed the alarm system and then led him into a large office on the first floor.

It was nicer than the offices had been at the law firm, done all in dark paneling and leather. It had a very old school feel to it.

Melinda went straight to a bookshelf, lifted a particular book, and retrieved a key that was there. She then moved over to the filing cabinet and unlocked it. She began to flip through the files while Mark walked around the office.

"Do you believe that Kent's accident was truly an accident?" he asked after a minute.

She froze, her shoulders bunching up. She finally said, "I thought it was at first. Just a terrible, terrible accident. But then I began to wonder. Something seemed off about it to me."

"What was that?"

"Well, for one, the area he was driving in. Everyone knows how treacherous that road is on a good day. In fog it's nearly impossible. And it was nowhere near his house. There was no way he would have taken it from his home to the office. He was going somewhere else or coming back from somewhere else. That's the only thing I could figure."

She took a deep breath. "No one wanted to talk about it, though, or pursue it. For a while I convinced myself that it was because it had to do with something confidential he or the firm had been working on for one of their clients."

"But you stopped thinking that?" Mark pushed.

"I started going through the files, one by one, looking for some reason why he might have been out where he was. I drew a complete blank, though. Nina caught me looking, too, and I had to make up some lame excuse. I think she's been watching me since then, though, just waiting for a chance to fire me. She's a strange one. It's like she lives for getting people into trouble."

"And yet her job is to get people out of it."

"Like I said, strange."

Mark had come to accept that anything that touched Not Paul's life had been strange.

"There's nothing under the Ds, but I'll keep looking," Melinda said, closing the top drawer of the filing cabinet and opening the next one.

Mark sat down at the desk and began to open drawers. It felt weird to do something like this without a search warrant. He kept telling himself that it was okay. Melinda had a key and Kent had authorized her to use it. Of course, that didn't extend to him. He'd just have to claim that he was with Melinda if they got caught.

He went through all the drawers on the right hand side with no success. Melinda moved down to the third drawer of the filing cabinet.

Mark switched to the drawers on the left hand side, but still had no luck identifying anything about Paul. A couple minutes later Melinda finished up with the filing cabinet and shook her head. "I've got nothing."

"Did he have a safe of any kind in here?" Mark asked.

Melinda frowned. "He does, but I don't think it will help."

"Do you know where it is and how to open it?"

She nodded and moved over to a large hunting picture on one wall. She swung it forward to reveal a wall safe behind it. "I know, it's terribly cliché, but what can you do? He was a traditional kind of guy."

"Let's hope he was traditional enough to leave something laying around that we can use," Mark said grimly.

The safe was a combination one and he stood back a couple of feet to give Melinda space. She spun the dials and a moment later was unlocking the safe.

Mark craned his neck to see what was in there. There appeared to be some cash, a couple pieces of jewelry, and a very small stack of folders.

The folders were what held Mark's attention. Without a word Melinda handed them to him. He took them and returned to the chair by the desk. He carefully spread them out, glancing at the titles of each one. The names were meaningless to him, but if they'd been placed in a safe instead of a filing cabinet, chances were they were important.

He flipped through the first four and put them aside. Then he came to the last one. Unlike the others it was labeled with only a single letter: P.

His hands began to shake as he opened up the folder. The first thing he saw was a picture of Paul, staring back at him.

9

Jeremiah and Cindy finally made it back to their bungalow after dinner. Once Jeremiah had done one more cursory sweep for bugs they settled down at the table to compare notes.

"Did you see this?" Cindy asked, holding up one of the brochures she had collected earlier.

"What is it?"

"Apparently they have a two week retreat once a quarter for those trying to beat gambling addictions."

"What's so strange about that?"

"It's just ironic, holding that kind of a retreat two miles down the road from a casino. I wonder how many people make a run for it?"

"I guess it depends on how serious they are about getting help. It does seem like an unnecessary temptation."

"Yeah, weird," Cindy said, dropping the brochure back onto the pile on the table.

"It's going to be an interesting week," Jeremiah commented.

"Yeah, maybe too interesting. I'm hoping we can get this solved so we can get out of here before we have to interact with some of those people again," Cindy admitted.

"Like the psychologist?"

"Yes! What was up with that? Did you see if he had a problem with anyone else besides you?"

"To be honest I couldn't tell. I was too busy focusing on each person we were talking to."

"He was seriously weird and seriously creepy. Of all the staff he and the guy running it are my picks for villains," Cindy said.

"They're the obvious choices given their behavior, but the question would be why? What would they have to gain by kidnapping or killing a retreat attendee?"

"I have no idea," Cindy said with a sigh.

"I think it's fairly safe to rule out anyone actually attending the couples' retreat unless we find out that someone was here for the other retreat as well."

"It's a good thing we can rule them out because otherwise there'd be just way too many suspects and people to point fingers at. Besides, some of them I wouldn't want to have to spend more time around them investigating."

"Like who?" Jeremiah asked.

Cindy rolled her eyes. "Jill and Kim for sure. I was so uncomfortable talking with them earlier. The two of them were busy obsessing over Dorothea and her pearl necklace. If that thing goes missing I know exactly where to look for it. I felt bad for their husbands. For something that's supposed to be a couples' retreat they gave zero focus to the men in their lives."

"That's okay, Jack and Levi were already plotting a prison break."

"How so?"

"They were trying to figure out when they'd have a chance to sneak away and hit the casino just down the road."

"Aha! Good thing they're not at the gambling addiction clinic. Although, maybe they should be."

"Apparently they're both big poker fans."

"I bet I could beat them," she mused.

"You play?"

"Yes, no, sorta."

"What does that mean?" he asked.

"I grew up playing with my father and my grandfather."

Jeremiah smiled. "I bet you took them for every penny."

Cindy laughed. "We played with poker chips for bragging rights. Although if we had played for pennies I would have gotten them all."

"I'd love to see you beat Levi and Jack. They seem to have pretty high estimations of their own skill. It'd be amusing to watch you deflate those egos a bit."

She shrugged. "Yeah, but they play for money. I've never done that. It's a different game when you actually have something to lose."

"That's true, but I still would love to see you beat them."

Cindy allowed herself a moment to picture that. It would be a sweet victory, especially if it upset their wives. She knew she wasn't being charitable, but both women had really rubbed her the wrong way. Dorothea, on the other hand, had seemed very sweet. Beth, the other woman at their dinner table, had been very quiet. So quiet that Cindy hadn't been able to get a good impression of her except to think that she must be even more introverted than Cindy could be.

"So, what is the plan for tonight?" she asked.

"I'm going to wait for midnight then slip out and see if I can break into the computer system and find out more about Malcolm, including which bungalow he was staying in."

"Okay, and what will I be doing?"

"Staying here and covering for me just in case we get any surprise late night visitors."

She blinked at him. "And just what do you think the odds of that happening are?"

"Late night visitors?"

"No, me staying here and doing nothing while you're out getting the information."

"I think the odds are pretty high," he said, narrowing his eyes. "I need you to be safe."

"Did you learn nothing over the summer?" she countered. "I'm safest when I'm with you."

"I think you'll be perfectly safe in this room. I don't want to put you in danger. I'm going to have to be moving fast and if I get caught I might be able to come up with a good excuse, but if they catch both of us it's over for sure."

As much as sneaking around the compound in the middle of the night sounded daunting and a little frightening to her, it was nothing compared to how she felt about waiting behind while he did all the sneaking around.

"I want to go, too."

"I don't think it's a good idea."

"I can help act as a lookout or something."

That made him smile for some reason. "Careful or you'll be offering to drive the getaway car next," he said.

She rolled her eyes at him. "We're breaking into a computer, not a bank vault. Besides, we don't have a car to drive."

"Okay, but we might want to rethink our wardrobes for the big caper. Matching black burglar costumes will be a little too suspicious."

"I think I have the perfect idea," Cindy said as something came to her. It was either brilliant or insane. Either way, she was running with it.

Mark stared at the image of his dead partner, feeling like he was looking at a ghost. His hands were shaking as he held the file folder. The picture was of Paul when he was younger, probably college-aged, standing with his arm around another guy's shoulders. They were both smiling for the camera.

"Did you find something?" Melinda asked, walking over to him.

"Paul. Do you know who the other guy in this picture is?" he asked.

"That's Kent. They both look so young there. It's hard to believe they're both gone," she said, her voice filling with sorrow.

"Tell me about it," Mark muttered.

He strained to see if he could make out any other details in the picture, but the background was blurry. He saw what were probably a couple of trees, but it could have been taken anywhere. He also wondered who had taken the picture.

"They were friends, I know that much. I always had the impression they met during their undergrad days," Melinda said.

Mark moved the picture and looked at the first page underneath it. At first he thought his eyes were playing tricks on him, then he thought the writing on the page must be in some foreign language. It took him several moments to realize he was staring at a coded message.

He instantly thought about the coded message Paul had had this man give to Georgia. Was it possible the two codes were the same?

"Did Kent ever write his more sensitive notes in code or a personal shorthand or something?"

"Not that I ever saw. Why?" Melinda asked.

He showed her the piece of paper. She took it and stared at it, frowning for a moment before handing it back. "I've never seen anything like this," she admitted.

There were at least a dozen pages in the file, all of them covered with the same unintelligible scrawl. Kent had written this in code, labeled the file with only a P and then locked it up in a safe. Whatever it was, he had done his best to keep it safe and hidden.

The hair lifted on the back of Mark's neck. Whatever it was, it could have gotten Kent killed.

He closed the file back up. "I'm going to take this with me," he said.

Melinda nodded slowly. "I don't see why not. The firm doesn't know the file is here. Kent's wife doesn't even know he has a safe in here. I think I was the only one who knew about it."

He thought of the key that Kent had given to Georgia. "There aren't any small boxes in that safe, are there?"

"No, just those files," she said.

Mark looked at the other files that had come out of the safe. He quickly flipped through the others. They all seemed to be tied to important people, but he didn't see anything like the code that was in Paul's file. Reluctantly he handed the other files back to her and she put them away.

"Kent didn't have any kind of safe deposit box, something a key would have gone to, did he?"

"If he did, he didn't tell me about it."

Given that Kent had trusted her with a key to his house and the combination to the safe even his wife didn't know he had she would have been the one to know something like that.

After she locked the safe back up and re-concealed it she turned to him. "Do you really think that file is going to help you?" she asked.

"I hope so. Are you really just going to leave those other files there? No one else knows they even exist."

"I know. He didn't want the firm to have them, so I never mentioned them, even after his death. I don't know what they are or what they pertain to, but I always figured if someone needed one of them really bad they'd come looking."

"Like I did," Mark said.

She nodded.

"And that's why you brought me here."

"Yes. I owe him that much."

"Someday others might come looking for those other files."

"I know."

"All of them might not be as friendly."

"I know that, too," she said. "But what else can I do?"

She was right. There was a reason the attorney had wanted those files kept safe. Turning them over to his firm or even to the police could be a huge mistake.

"I'll give you my card if you ever need help," he said.

"I appreciate that. And you have my number if there's anything more I can help with."

With nothing left to be said they left the house. Melinda set the alarm, locked the door, and moments later they were driving away. Once they got back to her house he'd be able to retrieve his rental car and make it back to the airport and get home in time for nighttime diaper duty. Traci would be pleased. She'd been right to urge him to fly. Had he driven up he would have missed seeing Melinda being escorted from the building and he wouldn't have the file he did now.

Mark realized he was clutching Paul's file so hard that the muscles in his hands were beginning to cramp. He'd have to figure out a way to break the code. Maybe he could enlist Jeremiah's help. Until he knew exactly what those pages said he wanted to be extremely careful who he shared them with. Deep in his gut he felt someone's life might depend on that.

"This is insane, you know that right?" Jeremiah whispered to Cindy as they let themselves into the building that held the registration desk.

"Or brilliant, it might be brilliant," she told him.

He wasn't sure how he'd let her talk him into this. It probably had a lot to do with the fact that he was banking on them not getting caught. Both of them had towels wrapped around them as though they were headed off to the pool for a midnight swim. While Cindy's logic had been somewhat sound, which was why he had ultimately given in, he felt completely exposed and vulnerable.

There was enough moonlight pouring in through the windows and glass doors that the interior of the building was lit in a soft glow. He positioned Cindy near the door where she could see out to the pathway leading up to the building. He had told her to let him know if she saw anything moving outside. The moon was shining brightly enough that they hadn't needed a flashlight when walking here which was good for them. It also meant someone else could sneak up on them fairly easily with no tell-tale bobbing light giving them away and that was bad.

With Cindy in position he moved over to the check-in counter and got behind it. He was gratified to see that whoever had last manned the station had simply shut off the monitor and not the entire computer. The screen blipped to life and he clicked on the icon for the reservation system. Fortunately it didn't ask for a password, a serious security flaw on their end. He spent about a minute figuring out his way around the program before he was able to do a search on past guests.

He typed in the name Malcolm Griffith and zero hits came back. It was possible Malcolm was actually a middle name he went by so he searched for the last name Griffith by itself. Zero hits still. He scowled. Just to make sure the system was actually working he typed in Flynn Castleback. More than a dozen entries instantly popped up. It seemed he and his wife really did spend their anniversary here every year.

He tried a different approach, searching instead by date range. He scrolled quickly through the names that came up but none of them were even similar to Malcolm Griffith.

Either he had been erased from their computer system or he had lied about being here in the first place. A good computer tech might be able to search the computer and find out if the records had been altered, but they didn't have access to someone like that.

He shut down the reservation program and was about to turn off the monitor when an icon on the desktop caught his eye. It was labeled Schedules.

He clicked on it and it popped up a workbook. There were tabs for different staff members. He clicked on the one for the psychologist, Dr. Carpenter. A spreadsheet with the days and times marked out and several boxes filled in with names came up. One of the boxes had his and Cindy's aliases filled in. He saw appointments for the others that they had met so far at the retreat.

He scrolled down past a black bar and he was suddenly looking at entries for the previous week. Apparently they kept the old schedules, at least for a while. Holding his breath he did a search for Griffith.

Malcolm Griffith had been scheduled for appointments with Dr. Carpenter on two different days. He had been scheduled to be here which meant he likely had been here. If he'd never shown up at the retreat center his information still should have come up in the reservation program showing whether he was charged a fee or refunded money or something. No, the fact that he was here in this file and missing from the reservation program told Jeremiah that Malcolm had been here and someone from the center had wanted to cover that fact up.

He also knew that given the first appointment with Dr. Carpenter had been scheduled prior to Malcolm's last phone call to his wife, the psychologist almost certainly had talked with him. Which meant they needed to talk to him.

Jeremiah closed down the program, shut off the monitor and moved over next to Cindy.

"Did you find anything?" she whispered.

"Yes, he was here but someone erased him from the system. They just didn't do a very thorough job of it," he said. "Are we all clear?"

"I haven't seen anyone."

"Okay, good."

They slipped out of the building, closing the door softly behind them, then hurried away from the building. They had only gone a dozen feet when Jeremiah heard a step and then a flashlight clicked on, shining right into their eyes.

10

Cindy squealed and grabbed onto Jeremiah's arm. She had planned to do that if they were caught, but she found that the reaction happened completely naturally. Her heart was pounding and she was so grateful that whoever it was hadn't come along when they were still inside the building.

"Where are you going?" an accented voice asked.

"The pool," Cindy said.

"You're a long ways from it." The flashlight lowered and she could see the Russian dance instructor staring at them.

"I told you we were going the wrong way to the pool. Would you listen? No!" she said, feigning anger, and hitting Jeremiah on the arm.

"What did you want me to do? Stop and ask for directions? From who? It's the middle of the freaking night," Jeremiah snapped.

"Well maybe you're not as eager to get to the pool as I thought you were."

"Come on, you know we would have gotten there and you would have chickened out...as usual."

"I might not have."

"Right. Then why are you wearing your bathing suit under the towel if you were actually planning on going skinny dipping?"

"In case we ran into anyone on the way there," she said, actually flushing at the thought of skinny dipping with Jeremiah.

"Okay, cool it you two," the big Russian said. "The pool's off limits after ten. And it's not okay to go skinny dipping at any time. And all this passion, frustration you're feeling, I suggest you save it for the dance floor. You're going to be sensational at the tango. Now, how lost are you? Do you need help finding your way back to your bungalow?"

"I think it's over there," Jeremiah said pointing in the wrong direction.

The dancer shook his head. "Which number?"

"Fourteen," Cindy said.

"Then you are all the way at the end, that way," he said, pointing past Jeremiah and slightly behind him.

"Thank you," Cindy said, trying to be as sincere as she could. "If it weren't for you we would have been tromping out here all night."

"It is my pleasure," the man said, giving her a slow, sexy grin.

"Let's go," Jeremiah said, grabbing Cindy's hand and pulling her in the direction of their bungalow.

"Goodnight, and thank you again," she called over her shoulder.

They hurried back to their bungalow and once inside Jeremiah turned to her with a frown. "You were flirting with him, that wasn't necessary."

"When a woman's mad at her boyfriend it's not unusual for her to flirt with someone else in front of him."

"To get his attention or punish him?"

"Probably a little of both," she admitted. "And if we were really lost and it was your fault of course I'd be grateful to him for helping out."

She paused and looked at him. "Are you okay?"

"Yeah, it just...bothered me is all."

"You were jealous?" she asked, unable to stop the grin that began to spread across her face.

"Yes," he admitted.

A little thrill rippled through her being. "How jealous?" she asked, taking a step closer to him.

"Jealous enough to punch his lights out."

She took two more steps so she was right in front of him and slid her arms up around his neck. "You know that you don't have to be jealous," she said, smiling up at him.

He stared at her a moment with a tortured look on his face even as she pressed closer to him.

"Cindy, don't," he said, his voice husky.

"Why? What's wrong?" she asked.

"Because unlike you I actually dressed the part. I'm not wearing swim trunks under this towel."

"Oh!" she said, letting go and quickly stepping back. For just a moment she thought she caught him smirking.

Jeremiah had no idea what had caused him to say that. It wasn't true, but the look on her face had been priceless. He was grateful, though, that she had moved away. Ever since they had run into the Russian he had found it impossible not to think about Cindy skinny dipping and it was playing havoc with his restraint. In a few minutes they would be getting ready to be going to sleep and the last thing he needed to be doing was thinking about her naked.

He went over, grabbed his pajamas and toiletry kit from his suitcase, and headed into the bathroom to change. When he was finished he exited back into the room. Cindy gave him a smile before disappearing into the bathroom with her things.

He sat down on the edge of his bed and took a few deep breaths. At least they had found out some good information tonight. It didn't put them any closer to finding out what had happened to Malcolm. At least, not yet, but it was a start.

He heard the shower go on in the other room and he closed his eyes in frustration. Once again he was thinking about water pouring off Cindy's skin. He laid back with a groan and tried to pray. They needed to wrap this up fast or it was going to be a very long week indeed.

When Cindy emerged from the bathroom Jeremiah appeared to be asleep. She was a bit relieved. It saved some potentially awkward conversation, particularly since all she could think about was the other two times she'd stayed overnight in any kind of hotel or resort with him and they'd had to share one bed. She found herself wishing that they hadn't been able to get a room with two beds in it and then scolded herself for the thought. Why did things between them have to be so complicated?

She turned off the light and got under the covers. As soon as she laid down she realized that she hadn't gotten a chance to ask Jeremiah what he'd found out about Malcolm and she felt instantly guilty. They were here to find a missing man and with every minute that passed that was going to be harder to do. Yet all she could think about was her relationship with Jeremiah.

Pull it together, Cindy, she scolded herself.

It didn't help her focus more when she reflected on the fact that since the beginning she'd been sure that what they were actually looking for was a dead body and not a kidnap victim. After all, if the man had been kidnapped surely his wife would have gotten some sort of ransom demand.

Unless like I did in Hawaii he stumbled into a situation and his kidnappers need him alive for some reason.

A brief wave of anxiety rolled over her. She hated remembering that experience. There had been so much pain, so much terror. She wouldn't wish that on anyone, especially a friend of someone she knew. What if Malcolm was like her? Desperately hoping that rescue was on its way but knowing that he would probably never be found?

Her stomach twisted in knots. If he was alive, he had to be found. They needed to stop wasting time.

She got out of bed and turned on the light. "Jeremiah, wake up!" she said.

He stirred and then rolled over and looked at her. "What's wrong?"

"Do you think Malcolm is dead?" she asked.

"I honestly don't know what to think. All I know is that he was here at some point."

"Then it's possible that he's still here."

"I guess. It's not exactly the ideal place to hold a hostage, but if whoever took him knew what they were doing it could be pulled off. And it might even be easier than trying to move him offsite without being seen."

"We have to check those other buildings, the staff only ones."

"Okay. In the morning we'll look at our schedule and see if we can find time to sneak over there."

"No, if he's alive then every second is crucial to keeping him that way. We need to go tonight."

"Are you serious?" he asked, blinking at her in surprise.

"Deadly serious. If he's alive we need to find him."

Jeremiah sat up. "If we go to those buildings we can't get caught. Not when they're so clearly off limits. No amount of blushing and bickering will get us out of that one."

"I know."

"If we're caught, that's it. They'll throw us out of here and there will be no one who can stop them from doing that."

She nodded. It was a huge risk, but so was every minute that they delayed. They could miss the opportunity to save Malcolm or the evidence they needed to catch his murderer could be destroyed. Either way time was of the essence.

"Okay, but I would feel a lot better if you stayed here with the door locked," he said.

She should agree with him. She *wanted* to agree with him. Earlier when she had been hovering near that door watching for signs that someone was about to spot them it had been completely nerve wracking. And despite her efforts they had been caught anyway.

"I know you would. And I would probably feel better, too, in some ways, but I can't. I can't stay while you go out."

"Why not?"

"Because I couldn't stand the fear of losing you again."

"Again?" he asked, frowning.

It felt like her chest was tightening, squeezing the breath out of her. She didn't want to talk about this. Not now. Not ever. She'd said it, though, the words were out there and he'd never understand if she didn't explain. She moistened her lips and cleared her throat before continuing.

"When we were in Iran, you let me think you were dead. I believed it and I had to live with it and those hours were the longest, worst hours of my life. Worse than my sister dying. Worse than my brother nearly dying. I was lost. And ever since then I've been afraid that you would die for real."

He reached out and grabbed her hand. "I'm not going to die."

"Can you promise me that?"

"I promise you, I'm not going to die," he said, staring down at their hands.

"Look me in the eyes and tell me that."

Jeremiah slowly raised his eyes to meet hers. "I promise you that I am not going to die tonight."

She took a deep breath, leaned forward and kissed him. "Thank you," she said as she pulled away. It did make her feel better even though she knew that he couldn't completely promise something like that. Aside from desperate kidnappers and murderers there were a lot of things that could hurt someone. Accidents happened.

She felt her heart skip a beat for a moment. She didn't want to go down that road in her mind. It was not a good road and it led to an even worse destination.

"So, it's agreed," he said. "I'll go alone."

Mark woke up to the sound of a baby crying. His brain was fuzzy as he turned his head to see the clock. It was nearly two in the morning. Traci was dead to the world, not even a twitch to show that she heard the crying. He didn't know how she did that. Every time one of the twins cried it woke him up, even if he knew it wasn't his turn to go check on them. Traci, however, managed to somehow lock into her subconscious when it was his night to handle things and she would never wake up. It baffled him and he would have given almost everything he owned to know how she did it so that he might replicate it.

He staggered out of bed. It was Ryan crying, he could tell. Ryan was a lot quieter in his crying than Rachel was. Rachel's cries were enough to wake the dead, which meant he really didn't know how Traci slept through it. Maybe she was undead, he thought. That was the only possible answer. Rachel was destined to grow up and be a scream queen with the set of lungs she had. Either that or a drill sergeant.

He winced as he entered the twins' room and the cries just became more piercing. Maybe when she got older he'd take her to work with him and see if she could outscream a police siren.

Ryan was awake, but quiet, just staring up with round eyes as Mark glanced at him. When Mark picked up Rachel she blessedly lowered her volume several notches. "What do you need, sweetheart?" he asked even though he suspected he already knew the answer.

He was so bleary-eyed and out of it that it took three times as long as it should have to get her into a fresh diaper. When he had finally put her back down he staggered out of the room, made it back to bed, and flopped down on it hard enough to make the bed shake.

Traci still didn't wake up. It was a good thing. She needed her rest. And yet some perverse part of him had the urge to reach over and shake her awake so that she would be suffering along with him in the moment.

He was grateful when the urge had passed because he knew that if he had actually given into it the most likely outcome would have been that he ended up with his eyes scratched out.

He closed his eyes and let his body relax back into the bed. He was so tired he was shocked he wasn't back asleep already. He waited for the sweet oblivion to claim him.

Fifteen minutes later he was still waiting. He tried flipping onto his side and readjusting his pillow. What was wrong with him? He wanted to sleep, he was desperate for it. His mind, however, had begun spinning, cataloguing the events of the day.

He couldn't get the coded papers out of his mind. When he'd gotten home he hadn't even had an opportunity to see if Kent and Paul's codes seemed similar. When he'd walked through the door he'd had just barely enough time to choke down some quasi-warm dinner before heading off to bed with Traci. She had been asleep the second her head touched her pillow so he hadn't even had a chance to discuss what he'd found with her.

Again he felt the urge to wake her up and again he managed to resist. It was possible that the papers he had discovered in Kent's files pertained to the truth of Paul's life and his real identity. That would make sense although he wouldn't have thought that Paul would have trusted anyone with his secrets. Is that why he'd put Kent through law school? Was it a bribe to keep his secrets? Attorney-client confidentiality could be a powerful thing and if Paul were to tell someone his secrets he'd want it to be someone who couldn't be called to testify against him. The two best candidates for that were a spouse or an attorney.

Even if that was what the papers were about, though, it didn't explain the key Paul had entrusted Kent to give Georgia. What could the key possibly lead to? If it was just papers confirming Paul's real identity, why bother? He could have instructed Kent to just tell Georgia the truth instead of sending her off to find heaven knew what with that key.

And the fact that the key had come with no instructions, just that coded message meant one of three things. Either Paul had expected Georgia to know or figure out what the key was for, or he had expected her to be able to decode his message, or he had expected her to bring Mark in to help.

Well Georgia certainly seemed clueless about the key just as he was. So that meant Paul must have been counting on either Georgia or Mark to be able to decode the note.

"Why couldn't you have just made it easy?" Mark whispered.

"Who are you talking to?" Traci said suddenly and loudly enough to make him jump.

"That? That you wake up for?" he asked incredulously.

"It sounded important."

"It is. I found some more things out about Paul, but they've only led to more questions than answers. Now I'm left with a bunch of coded papers, a key that fits heaven knows what, and no idea what to do with either of them."

Traci didn't say anything.

"Hon?"

Silence.

"Hon, you still awake?" he said, significantly louder.

She snored softly and he rolled his eyes. If he wanted to talk to Traci he was going to have to wait for morning.

From the other room Ryan began to softly cry.

Jeremiah was on edge as he snuck from building to building. He honestly didn't think he would find Malcolm, or anything that would lead them to Malcolm. It was possible, though, that he'd stumble onto something questionable or downright illegal. If he did that might provide a motivation for someone to have gotten rid of Malcolm if he'd discovered the same thing. As long as no one tried to get rid of Jeremiah or Cindy, everything should be fine.

The only building he'd steered clear of appeared to house some sleeping quarters for staff members staying on overnight. It made sense. There were no activities late at night and no expectation that guests would need anything, but having staff at least present in case of an emergency was smart. Plus he was pretty sure that they took turns patrolling the grounds at night. He had managed to avoid running into the dance instructor as he met up with the yoga instructor outside the dormitory and handed her a set of keys and the flashlight. Jeremiah noticed that both of them were incredibly light on their feet so he knew he'd have to stay alert and not trust to his ears to give him warning of their approach.

The final building appeared to just be a storage facility. There were all manner of items from extra yoga mats to cases of toilet tissue. One wall was even lined with canned foods, the kind that could keep for a long time. He moved through the building, using the flashlight app on his phone to get a better look at some things.

On the far right side toward the back he encountered a door which was locked. He reached into his pocket for tools to help him pick it. Just as he was starting to insert the first metal instrument into the lock he froze.

Something wasn't right. He could feel it. He held his breath, the better to listen. Then he heard it, a very soft footfall. There was someone else in the building and that person was headed straight for Jeremiah.

11

Jeremiah turned off his phone and shoved it in his pocket. For a split second he thought about going ahead and picking the lock on the door and then hiding in whatever space was behind it. It was too risky, though. He probably had just enough time, but if the door's hinges creaked at all it would give him away.

He glided back the way he'd come, trying to remember everything he'd seen in the front part of the building. One window in the building high up on the side was letting in just enough moonlight to keep him from tripping over anything in the dark.

He had nearly made it to the front door when he heard the knob twist and the door begin to open. He backpedaled, realizing he was caught between two different people. He looked at the pallets of toilet paper that were stacked on top of each other and realized there was just enough room between them and the wall for him to squeeze in.

He moved quickly but carefully, making sure not to knock into anything. He reached the pallets and wedged himself behind them then crouched down with one foot on the floor and one on the edge of the bottom pallet. It was an awkward position and he had to brace himself with one hand against the wall.

He heard the front door close and then footsteps, these much louder than the ones that had been coming from the back of the building. The speaker clearly felt confident of his reason to be in the building.

The footsteps stopped not five feet from Jeremiah's hiding place. He tensed, readying himself to spring out if need be even though he was fairly certain his presence had not yet been discovered.

"Hello," a male voice called out in a loud whisper.

"There you are," came an even quieter response. The second voice was definitely female. "Isn't it a little early to be having this conversation?"

"I thought we should get started. I think we have some interesting prospects this time around."

"Like that old couple?"

"No, we need to leave the regulars alone," the man said firmly. "Besides, those two strike me as inseparable."

"Then who do you have in mind?"

"Jack and Levi. I have a feeling we could get them in a heartbeat."

"And I don't think their wives would even notice until it was too late," the woman said.

Jeremiah was struggling to believe his good fortune in happening into this building in time to overhear this conversation. He thought about Cindy's sudden insistence that they not wait any longer to check out the other buildings. Maybe G-d had been prompting her. He was grateful that she had stayed back in their room, though. He would never have known that the woman was in the back of the building, in the dark, waiting for someone. He and Cindy probably would have spoken or made some sound that would have alerted her and ruined everything.

The question now was, what did these two think that Jack and Levi were likely candidates for? The woman was right about one thing, Jill and Kim certainly weren't paying very close attention to their husbands thus far at the retreat and they could likely be gone for hours before they were even missed.

He still wasn't sure who the two speakers were, but he dared not risk trying to get a look at them at this point. They were so close they would almost certainly catch the movement if he peeked out from behind the pallets.

"Any other likely prospects?" she asked.

"I'm not sure yet. Things should get a lot clearer tomorrow when we have a chance to really work with them."

So, they definitely were staff members. He'd been certain that was the case, but it was nice to have confirmation. Now he just had to figure out which ones. If he couldn't get a good look at them or if they didn't raise their voices louder than a whisper then he'd have to spend the next day watching to see who was watching the guests.

"Are you sure it's safe, doing this again so soon?" she asked.

"I'm positive," the man said. "What happened last time was a fluke. And besides, no one can touch us here."

Jeremiah wondered if the last time that they were discussing had involved Malcolm. If so, it hadn't gone the way they expected things to go.

For a moment Jeremiah considered leaping out from his hiding place and confronting them. It would certainly be the faster way to get things done. It could also prove highly problematic. They weren't likely to spontaneously confess to anything. He wasn't a police officer so he couldn't just arrest them, and on what little he'd overheard Mark would never be able to come onto the reservation to arrest them.

Even if he could there wasn't near enough evidence of any kind of wrongdoing to be of use.

Of course, he could threaten or otherwise force a confession, but he knew it wouldn't hold up in court if they confessed under duress. Besides, he didn't yet know if anyone else was involved, and he didn't want to risk letting any co-conspirators get away.

Whatever was going on here he'd have to get more information before he or Mark could do anything. He also noted that separating couples from each other was an essential element to their plans. Which meant that aside from being watchful he'd need to stick to Cindy like glue.

"Keep your eyes open tomorrow. We'll meet again tomorrow night to talk more," the man said.

"Okay, but not here, please. This building always gives me the creeps after dark," she said.

"I don't know why you're always so jumpy. It's just a storeroom."

"Yeah, but you weren't in here earlier. There were noises."

"Like what?"

"I don't know, just noises. Creaking sounds I guess."

"It's a building. They do that at night."

"Yeah, but for a minute I could swear you were here before you actually came in."

"What do you mean?"

"I don't know. It was like there was another presence in here."

"Now you're just losing it. You've been watching too many episodes of that ghost hunting show on the Escape! channel."

"I have not."

"Fine. Look, I'll figure out somewhere else we can meet tomorrow night. Now let's go before someone catches us in here."

When he heard footsteps moving toward the front door, Jeremiah risked standing, trying to get a look at them. It was no use, though. It was too dark to even make out hair color or anything else significant about either of them.

He heard the door open and close. He waited a minute then made his way to the back of the building to see if there was anything he hadn't been able to see in that area before.

It was fortunate that the man had been so dismissive of her concerns, particularly about feeling a presence in the building. If he'd been at all smart he would have at least done a cursory investigation before writing her and her feelings off the way he did.

Jeremiah went through the rest of the building but didn't find anything suspicious. When he made it back to the front he stood for a moment with his ear against the door. He couldn't hear any sound from the outside so he slowly opened the door and slipped out, closing it behind him.

He made his way swiftly and quietly back to the bungalow. He didn't run into any patrolling staff members which was a relief.

When he walked into the room Cindy got up from where she'd been sitting at the table, ran over, and hugged him tight.

"I was so worried!"

"I'm okay. I'm here," he said, lightly stroking her back.

She finally pulled away and moved to take a seat on her bed. "Did you find anything?" she asked.

"Nothing tangible, and no sign of Malcolm, but I did overhear two staff members conspiring together."

"What about?"

"That's the thing. I'm not entirely sure."

He quickly filled her in on what he'd overheard. She listened intently and when he was finished she sat silent for a moment.

"Any thoughts?" he asked.

"Do you think they're only targeting men?" she asked.

"I'm not sure. It's possible they're targeting a certain profile and it just so happens that the initial obvious candidates are men. Of course, they lumped Dorothea and Flynn together. That could have been deliberate or just them being imprecise."

"They have money, but I don't know how well off Jack and Levi are in that area."

"It might be worth finding out. I know Mark had mentioned that Malcolm was wealthy."

"I would almost think that whatever they're doing, Malcolm couldn't have been the first," she said.

"Given what they said and how they said it, I came to the same conclusion."

"Do you think Mark can track down some of the former guests here and see if anything strange happened to them?"

"Not without a list of who has been a guest," Jeremiah said. "I might be able to get him one off of the computer system."

Cindy nodded. "Before we risk that, let's talk to him."

"Agreed."

"So, what now?"

"I think we should get some sleep. I have a feeling we're going to need to be on our toes tomorrow."

Jeremiah and Cindy sat on pillows, legs crossed, facing each other. They were less than an arm's length apart and the first thing Jeremiah noticed was that it promoted an immediate feeling of intimacy. It also meant that they were invading each other's personal space. He had been closer to her before, holding her, kissing her. They had rarely been this close in public, though, except for the occasional quick hug.

He had to remind himself that no one was looking at them. Everyone in the room was busy looking at their own partner. He still felt like they were on display, though, for all the world to see. It made him uncomfortable.

He wasn't ready for their relationship to be public. Once people knew that they were dating it would change so many things. It would also put incredible pressure on both of them. Disapproval was bound to come from both sides. While some couples might just have to deal with friends and family, Cindy and he had to concern themselves with the synagogue and church families that they worked for. While not families in the strictest sense of the word, they tended to act like families with all the good and the bad that came with that. He was fairly certain they wouldn't be getting much, if any, support from the synagogue. He suspected that it would be the same for the church.

If they both had different jobs, different lives, they could hold their breaths and wait out the storm. The problem was, they didn't. He was the rabbi, the spiritual leader of the synagogue and expected to set an example. He could already hear what people were going to say. It didn't help that he'd already gotten a taste of it both from Marie and from his family in Israel.

Cindy worked for the church. It was only a matter of time before someone decided to object to paying the salary of someone who was dating outside the faith. In his mind he pretty much was sure how things would ultimately play out. The only question was, which one of them would get fired first?

"What's wrong?" Cindy asked, frowning as she stared at him.

"It's nothing. Sorry, just lost focus there for a moment," he said.

He was stressing out too much. He needed to just slow down and handle one problem at a time. And the problem at hand was figuring out what had happened to Malcolm.

For this first large group session Arnold was in charge and he was walking around the perimeter of the room as everyone got settled, urging different couples to sit closer together. By chance the closest couple to them was Dorothea and Flynn. Other familiar faces weren't that far away. Whether or not that was by accident or design, he wasn't sure.

Cindy was wearing another new looking outfit. She was wearing a turquoise silk tank top and white shorts that were very short by her standards. With her legs crossed it made the shorts seem even shorter. He'd certainly never seen as much of her legs as he was staring at now.

She wasn't the only woman in the room in shorts. It was a pretty warm day for February. On top of that the buildings were temperature controlled which meant that it was very comfortable inside.

"Alright, everyone, we're going to start by spending an entire minute staring into your spouse's eyes. Don't say anything, just look. Don't break the eye contact. It might be intimidating, but trust me the shared vulnerability is a good thing. I will tell you when you can stop, and it will seem like longer than a minute has passed, but I assure you it won't have. Alright, look each other in the eyes beginning now."

Jeremiah stared into Cindy's eyes. She was smiling back at him for the first several seconds. Color began to creep into her cheeks slowly and it made her look a bit more agitated. He could relate. He didn't often allow himself the luxury of staring at her this intently. When he did it always brought so many emotions to the surface.

Cindy was biting her bottom lip now. He wondered what she was thinking about.

After what seemed like an eternity Arnold spoke up. "Okay your minute is over. Now I noticed some of you followed directions while others seemed to be having a hard time with simple instructions. Don't worry, you get another shot at doing this right. This time I want you to picture the person across from you as they were when you first met and fell in love with them. Don't think of everything that has happened since. Ignore the wrinkles, the gray, the fights you seem to repeat over and over. Just look at them and see the person you first connected with. Ready, go."

It was hard to look at Cindy now and think of how she had been when they met. She had been so timid, so afraid back then. Since then, though, she'd been evolving into a tigress. As to when or how he'd fallen in love with her, he couldn't say. It had just happened. A thousand tiny moments had come together to build something strong and powerful.

He had helped change Cindy. He knew that. But she had done just as much to change him. Because of her he had friends that were like family. He belonged. And he was willing to risk getting hurt by being close to her.

"Okay, very good, now say the first thing that comes to mind," Arnold said, his voice interrupting the spell.

"I love you." Cindy, Jeremiah, Flynn, and Dorothea had all said it at the same time. With his sharp hearing Jeremiah could also make out a few other similar sentiments around the room. Some of the other things spoken, though, surprised him.

"You blinked first. I win."

"Did you remember to turn the stove off?"

"Well, that was awkward."

"I think you're getting gray hairs in your eyebrows. Can you dye those?"

"Dang, you've gained a lot of weight."

"I told you this was going to be stupid."

It was a mixture of male and female voices that had less than romantic things to say to their significant other. It was bewildering. Although he thought for a moment he caught Cindy smirking at a couple of them.

"Remember, this is not a competition. Not between each other and not with the other couples," Arnold chided gently.

"If it was, we'd totally be winning," Cindy whispered.

Jeremiah barely held back a laugh. He'd just been thinking the same thing.

"Actually, I think you'll find we're winning," Flynn whispered next to Jeremiah.

Jeremiah turned and regarded the older man who had an impish look on his face.

"No way!" Cindy whispered, barely keeping her voice down.

"Care to bet on it?" Flynn asked.

"Okay, that's enough. Please don't bet him. He likes to bet on everything and he usually wins," Dorothea said. "Honestly, it still amazes me sometimes that on our first trip here I didn't lose him to the casino."

"Okay, settle down everyone," Arnold said. "It's not social time, it's work time."

Dorothea actually giggled like a schoolgirl and Flynn whispered, "I don't think that word means what he thinks it means."

Without warning a piercing wail filled the building.

12

Cindy jumped, startled, as the alarm ripped through the air, shredding whatever sense of calm and tranquility had been present. She glanced up at Arnold who looked completely startled. She watched him quickly pull himself together.

Arnold clapped his hands together twice. "Alright everyone, this is a fire drill. Please move quickly and safely to your nearest exit and meet me outside under the large palm tree."

Jeremiah was on his feet in a flash, and, after giving Cindy a hand up, he turned and helped Dorothea and Flynn up as well. Together they exited through one of the sliding glass doors and moved to the palm tree where they were the first to arrive.

"In all the years we've been coming here we've never had to do a fire drill," Dorothea said.

"Maybe it's a new policy," Cindy said, not wanting to worry the other woman.

One thing was clear to her. Arnold had been just as startled as everyone else in that room when the alarm went off.

Is it a false alarm or is there actually a fire somewhere on the property? she wondered.

She could tell Jeremiah was wondering the same thing. She reached out and took his hand. He closed his around hers and it made her feel safe and secure. Warmth flooded through her as it always did at his touch.

"Mark, you okay?"

A hand descended on Mark's shoulder and he jumped. He looked up and saw Liam standing over him, an amused look on his face. "Diaper duty last night?" Liam asked.

"How can you tell?" Mark asked with a yawn.

"Well, you're usually not in the habit of falling asleep at your desk for one thing."

"The twins kept tag teaming all night. You know, I swear sometimes they do it on purpose, but just when it's my night to deal with it. They never do that to Traci on her nights."

Liam chuckled. "You think they're plotting against you now, wait another year or two. Then you'll be in real trouble."

"Thank you so much for that," Mark said sarcastically.

"Is that paper on your desk that didn't manage to hold your attention urgent?"

Mark glanced down. "No, it's a department memo. You've probably got a copy on your desk. You know that tech guy up in northern California who killed his wife last year, and it was all in the news for weeks?"

"Jason Todd? What about him?"

"Apparently they can't put together a jury pool up there because there was too much press."

"And everyone already thinks he's guilty?"

"Exactly. Looks like they're going to move the trial down here."

"When?"

"End of next month."

"And why are we getting a memo about it?"

"The department's been advised by our colleagues up north that there's a high likelihood that there are going to be demonstrators."

"Lovely," Liam said with a frown.

"Yeah, I guess they can't move this guy two feet without people getting wind of it and showing up. There's also already been two assassination attempts against him."

"So now it gets to be our problem."

"Exactly. So, apparently a plan is being worked up to handle things once he gets down here. They'll keep us informed as we get closer, etc., etc."

"Sounds like a good time to take vacation."

"It would be, but the captain's already put his foot down on that one. No one's going anywhere."

"Thank you northern California for that," Liam said, rolling his eyes. "Have you had breakfast yet?"

"Is it a bad thing if I tell you that I can't honestly remember?"

"Yes, come on, let's get out of here for a while."

Mark followed Liam outside. In the parking lot he yawned again.

"I think I should drive," Liam said.

"Good idea," Mark told him as he handed over the keys.

Ten minutes later they were sitting down in a coffee shop. As soon as they'd ordered Liam leaned forward.

"So, what did you find yesterday?" he asked.

"Quite a lot," Mark admitted. "Unfortunately all of it just led to more questions and no answers."

Liam nodded slowly, frowning as he did so.

"What is it?" Mark asked.

"You figured out a while back who Paul really was, didn't you?"

"Yeah, I got his birth name and a rough idea of what his life was like before he assumed the other kid's identity."

"So, here's what I don't understand. What are you looking for now? You got the answers you set out to find after his death."

"Traci has asked me the same thing."

"Then what's the deal?"

"I guess I just don't feel like the case is closed, at least, not for me."

"Maybe what you really mean is that you haven't personally found closure. That's not the same thing."

"I know that," Mark said, feeling defensive. "And you're right, I haven't, but there's more to it than that."

"Then tell me what it is," Liam urged.

Mark sighed. "I think Paul's real father is still out there somewhere. The man needs to be brought to justice for his crimes."

"Agreed, but how do you plan on pulling that off? You're not with the F.B.I., you're a Pine Springs cop. You don't have the resources to track this man across the country if he still even exists. And the trail is so cold at this point that there's very little use in trying."

"I know that, but it still keeps me up at night sometimes. Then, yesterday, something happened. His widow came to me with a coded piece of paper and a key that a lawyer had delivered to her after Paul didn't show up for his annual meeting. After months of having no clue what to do with them, she gave them to me."

Liam frowned. "So, he had an annual meeting with this lawyer and had given him instructions to pass these things on if something happened to him and he failed to attend one of those meetings?"

"Apparently so."

"That sounds like the threat people are always making in movies. 'If anything happens to me, this all goes public' sort of thing."

"I know."

"So, what did the message say?"

"I don't know. I'm going to need some time to figure out how to decode it. I'm hoping it will give me some clue about the key, because I haven't the foggiest notion where to start on figuring out what it goes to."

"And the evidence you were worried about yesterday that could have been destroyed?"

"I'm not sure it wasn't. It turns out the attorney who gave her those things was killed in a car accident. When I started asking questions one of the partners at the firm began shredding documents and fired the guy's assistant."

"Would she be the one I tracked down yesterday?"

"Yes, thank you. She led me to where the attorney kept files he didn't want others to see. One of them had a picture of Paul in it and pages of writing in that same code. Apparently they were friends since college."

Liam whistled low. "You need to get on cracking that code as soon as possible."

"I know."

"What do you think the attorney's pages contain, an account of Paul's identity and real life? Or maybe he's just the tip of the iceberg."

"That's what I need to figure out."

Liam nodded. "Well, I'll help you in any way I can."

"Thanks, I need all the help I can get. Know any good code breakers?"

"Sadly, no. My grandfather was, but I never got the chance to learn anything from him."

"Is this the same grandfather who was the gun collector?" Mark asked.

"Yup."

"He had to be an interesting guy."

Liam just smiled.

Mark's phone chimed and he pulled it out of his pocket. Traci had sent a text asking if he could pick up a few things at the grocery store on his way home. He replied that he would.

"It looks like I missed a call from Jeremiah," he said.

"Must have been while you were sleeping."

The rabbi had left a message and Mark played it.

It's me. I need to know if M's wife knows what room he was in. Also, can you tell us if M was a wealthy man?

Mark called back but it went to voicemail. He waited for the beep and then said, "As to your first question, I'll find out. To your second, yes, he was a rich man," and hung up.

Liam started chuckling.

"What?" Mark asked.

"For a moment there I thought you were going to break into a song from *Fiddler on the Roof*."

"That would have amused you too much."

"So, you're going to deprive us both of the pleasure of you singing?"

"No, I'm saving us both from my singing. One day you'll thank me for it, trust me."

136

He called the station and a minute later was talking to the captain.

"Hi, it's Mark. Jeremiah and Cindy want to know if we know which room Malcolm was staying in."

"Why, have they found something?"

"Not that I'm aware of, but apparently they need to know the room."

"Yes, his wife told me when she brought this all to my attention. Let me grab my notes."

Mark could hear the sound of pages being flipped through in a notebook. Finally the captain picked the phone back up. "Bungalow nine. He always gave her his room number when he was staying somewhere, just in case."

"Thanks, I'll pass it on."

"Call me the moment they know anything."

"I will," Mark promised. He hung up and called Jeremiah again.

"Nine," he said when the voicemail came on.

He hung up just as their food arrived.

Jeremiah had felt his phone go off twice while they were waiting to go back inside the building. When they finally got the go ahead he lingered behind for a quick moment and checked his messages. They were both from Mark and were short and to the point.

He deleted them and then moved to catch up with the others. "Bungalow nine and rich," he whispered in Cindy's ear.

She nodded to indicate that she understood.

For the rest of the morning session he noticed that both of them had trouble focusing. It was with relief that they headed out when dismissed. They had about twenty minutes before lunch was served so they quickly made their way back to their bungalow to discuss what to do next.

As soon as the door had closed behind them Cindy turned to Jeremiah. "Bungalow nine, isn't that Tristan and Beth's room?"

"Yes."

"Well, how are we going to break in there and search for clues?"

"I've been thinking about that," Jeremiah said. "Whoever was involved with his disappearance erased him from the reservation system. We can assume they also went through the trouble of going through the room carefully when getting rid of his stuff. So, I doubt that barring a full forensics sweep of the room we will turn up anything of note."

"So, what do we do then?"

"We make them think they missed something. Then we watch to see who responds. I'm guessing that whatever they did with his stuff, they didn't just toss it in one of the dumpsters. They probably thought of a better way to dispose of it and hopefully we can trick them into trying to do the same with the evidence we manufacture."

"What did you have in mind, exactly?"

"I think our man Malcolm left a journal with some very interesting things written in it. The only question is, where do we get a journal?" Jeremiah mused.

Cindy went instantly over to the closet and opened her bag. A moment later she returned with a brown leather notebook in hand. He took it from her in surprise and noted with relief that it was blank inside.

"How did you just happen to have this?" he asked.

She shrugged. "The only retreats of any kind I've been to they've always had us bring our Bible and a journal to write in. I brought both here. Habit I guess."

"You are a genius," he said with a grin.

"Thanks. How do you know that whoever is behind his disappearance won't just burn it or something?"

"We need to put something compelling in there that will force their hand, make them go check him or the things that were in his room."

"Or maybe both in case they can't get to one but they can get to the other," Cindy suggested.

"Good idea." He glanced at the clock. "It's time for lunch. We can think about what we want to write and then set our plan in motion just before dinner. We'll just need a way to get Tristan and Beth to find the book and turn it in."

"Oh, I'm already working on a plan for that," Cindy said.

"Good."

They went and had a quick lunch. When they returned Jeremiah sat down and began to make fake journal entries for the first couple of days of Malcolm's stay at the retreat center. While he mentioned the names of a couple of the staff he made sure to leave things generic enough that no one would be able to tell that the entries were faked.

Cindy fished some resort stationery out of a drawer and handed it to Jeremiah.

"What do you want me to do with this?" he asked.

"I want you to write a letter from Malcolm to his wife. Then we're going to seal it up in an envelope addressed to her and put it inside the journal."

"What do you want me to say?"

"Tell her that you have a bad feeling about something and that just in case you want her to know that the combination to your briefcase is I don't know, make up some numbers, and that you've got some money or something in there. Also that you've got a diamond hidden in the heel of your one shoe. You know how paranoid you always are about being caught somewhere with no access to your money, but you want her to be able to recover these things in case something happens, etc."

"Aha, so they'll need to check his shoes, which are hopefully with him, and his briefcase which might not be. Excellent thinking. That's better than what I was coming up with."

"Thank you," she said with a grin.

He barely had time to finish the letter and seal it in the envelope before they had to head to their afternoon sessions. He slid the book underneath the mattress just in case anyone came in while they were gone. It wasn't the most secure place in the world, but at least it wasn't sitting out in the open.

By the time Mark made it home he was exhausted. He was home early which should make Traci happy. He just hadn't been able to keep it together any longer. On the way home he nearly fell asleep twice and it was not a long drive. He'd only barely remembered to pick the things up at the store she'd requested.

The house looked so peaceful when he pulled up into the driveway and he sat in his car a moment, just drinking it in. He had hoped to spend some time tonight going over the coded pages and seeing if he could discover anything about them. That just wasn't in the cards, though. He was, however, immensely grateful that it was Traci's turn to be on diaper duty.

He got out of the car and somehow made it to the front door, dragging his feet more with each step. He unlocked it, walked inside, and saw Traci in the kitchen, working away.

He closed the door, took a step forward, and right as Traci turned around he saw sparks flashing behind her and then something exploded.

13

Mark shouted as Traci screamed and covered her head. Mark lunged past her as he realized the source of the sparks. He turned off the microwave and yanked the door open. The husks of what might have been baked potatoes sat empty, their insides vaporized. They rested on top of a serving plate with fine gold metallic decorations around the border.

He turned to look at Traci who ran to him, threw her arms around his neck, and broke down sobbing. He held her in stunned silence, not sure what to say.

"I'm sorry, I'm so sorry," she finally managed to get out amidst the sobs.

"It's not your fault, honey. It was an accident," he said.

He was stunned, though. He'd never known her to have any kind of kitchen mishap let alone one involving metal in the microwave.

"All the dinner plates were dirty and I knew I had to hand wash two for dinner, and I just couldn't handle washing one more, and I thought I'd use a serving plate."

"And you didn't realize the one you grabbed had metal on it."

"I forgot. I'm forgetting so much lately."

"It's okay. We both are. It's because our sleep schedules have been interrupted for so long. We'll get through this, though. Rachel and Ryan won't be infants forever."

"I can't be on diaper duty tonight, I just can't," she said, continuing to cry.

Mark winced. He had been counting on her handling that tonight since he was the walking dead. Instead he heard himself saying, "It's okay, I can do it tonight."

He glanced once more at the microwave, wondering how on earth the contents of the two potatoes had managed to vaporize. He'd seen a lot of frightening things in all his years as a cop, but that gave him the creeps.

"Why don't we go sit down on the couch?" he suggested.

Traci nodded and he led her over there and sat down with her. She sank onto his chest and he held her. They were both so frazzled and they needed some time just for themselves.

"I was thinking that we need to get a babysitter so we can go out, just the two of us, for Valentine's Day," he said, hoping the thought would cheer her up.

Apparently he had guessed wrong as she started sobbing harder. He was bewildered, wondering how what he had suggested could be making things worse.

Finally Traci looked up at him. "I called everyone already and no one can do it."

There was so much anguish on her face that he knew he had to do something, even if it was drastic. He chose his next words carefully. "I know we said we'd always just use friends and family, but I know there is a very reputable service that some of the guys at work have told me about, and the babysitters are all thoroughly screened, the works."

"I already called them and everyone's booked," Traci said.

He was stunned to hear that. Even more than he, Traci had been adamant about not letting strangers take care of their children. It just went to show how desperate she was.

"Well, you know what, to heck with Valentine's Day. I say we make our own Valentine's Day. We'll take off the weekend after, just the two of us, and have a little getaway. I'm sure we can twist someone's arm into helping out after the holiday."

"You mean it?" Traci asked.

"Of course I do. I'll make all the arrangements, unless you want to pick where we're going."

"No, I don't want to have to think or worry about one more thing. I'm sick of making a thousand decisions every day. I just want to forget it all and relax."

"Then that's exactly what you're going to do." He kissed the top of her head. "Don't worry, it will all be just fine."

She settled down and leaned her head on his shoulder, her tears drying up. He sat with his arm around her, offering whatever support and comfort was his to give. It was some kind of miracle that they hadn't heard a peep from the twins during the entire meltdown.

"There's a Valentine's Day dinner at Cindy's church. She said a lot of families go to it," Traci said after a minute. "So, there'll be a lot of other kids, but at least we could go out."

"Then let's do that," he said.

"Okay."

She was sounding a lot calmer. Not calm enough yet for him to be able to make a joke about the microwave, but definitely getting there.

As if she couldn't stand not being the center of attention any longer Rachel let out a piercing scream from the other room. It was so loud and sudden that it made both Mark and Traci jump.

He thought about sitting still and praying that she would just decide to stop. A second blast, though, forced him up onto his feet and had him heading for the nursery.

Yoga and a small group session had been okay although Cindy felt like she'd been turned into a bit of a pretzel in the one and a knot of tension in the other. Their last afternoon session before dinner was with Dr. Carpenter, which would likely prove interesting.

They walked into Dr. Carpenter's office. The dominating feature of the room was a big, comfy looking leather sofa. There was also a cherrywood desk, some file cabinets, and an equally comfortable looking leather chair that he was sitting in behind his desk. He was hunched over, intently studying some papers, and he did not lift his eyes.

"We will begin in one minute. First I will talk to each of you individually for fifteen minutes. Then I will talk to you both for thirty minutes. I will start with the woman first. The other one may wait outside until it is his turn."

His word choice totally stunned and offended Cindy. "We do have names, you know?"

"Do you? We shall see," he said, without looking up from the papers on his desk.

"I don't want to go first," Cindy objected, feeling rattled and more than a little creeped out.

"And yet you will go first because that is the way in which it is done."

She turned to look at Jeremiah expecting to see him look as angry as she was. Instead his face was an absolute blank. She stared at him. How did he do that? She remembered that for the longest time it had been nearly impossible to read any of his emotions. She realized now that because of who he was and all his training that he had made an active effort to emote, particularly around her.

She appreciated it. Staring at him and not being able to get the least little hint as to what he was thinking or feeling was unnerving.

"You'll be fine. I'll be right outside," Jeremiah said, his voice completely neutral.

She wanted to punch him in the arm because his tone did nothing to calm her down. She refrained, though, and went and sat on the couch. Jeremiah closed the door, sealing her in with the psychologist.

"Let's get this over with," Cindy said.

"Not for another 15 seconds," he chided.

"Are you kidding me?"

"I never joke about time. Timing is everything, especially in relationships."

"What do you mean?"

"One second you meet, another second you do not. You meet at the right time and you fall in love. You meet at the wrong time and you don't. At the right time you can establish a relationship. At the wrong time you cannot. And when things begin to fall apart at the right time you can speak the words that will save it while at the wrong time you can't."

He finally looked up at her. "And this is now the right time to figure out where you and your boyfriend are, timewise." He leaned back in his chair. "So, tell me, why do you love your boyfriend?"

"That's none of your business," Cindy snapped.

"Ah, but it is very much my business and this is the time for you to find out if the relationship works for you. My dear, believe it or not I am on your side," he said, his voice softening a little at the end.

Cindy took a deep breath. "He's strong, smart, thoughtful, spiritual, fun. I feel safe when I'm with him."

"And what happened to you as a child that feeling safe is such a driving force for you?"

She stared at him in surprise. "What makes you think something happened to me?"

"Because the first characteristic of his that you listed was that he was strong. And the thing that he makes you feel is safe. You didn't say that he makes you feel excited or alive, loved or appreciated, ready to take on the world, supported or respected, or even beautiful. You said he makes you feel safe. That means that safety is a number one concern for you and the only people who have that as their number one concern in life are those who have felt truly unsafe in the past, generally as a result of something traumatic that happened to them as a child."

"I, I thought I had gotten over my need to be safe," Cindy blurted out, shocked at the revelation.

"No, my dear, you haven't. You've just redefined safety for yourself and you've chosen this man to be your protector. You still have as great a need for safety as ever, but now you associate being with him as what keeps you safe. This allows you to probably engage in a great many more activities that have an element of risk in them than you once would have. You engage in these activities with confidence, not because you no longer need to feel safe but because as long as he is there you believe that you are safe regardless of what you're doing."

He was right. She knew it, felt it. Deep down she was still a scared little girl, but she'd found someone who she could trust to worry about her safety so that she didn't have to.

"There is, on the surface, nothing wrong with finding a man who fulfills this need for you. We are all looking for life partners to fulfill particular needs. What we must keep in mind, though, particularly with someone like you who has an incredibly strong need for one thing in particular, is that we cannot sacrifice everything else to that need."

"What are you saying?" Cindy asked.

"You need to feel safe. Being with this man makes you feel safe. Because you don't want to lose him, or lose the safety he represents to you, there is a temptation to not rock the boat so to speak, to let other needs go unfulfilled because you're afraid that if you push, you'll lose him. For you it's safety first and you sacrifice everything else to that."

That had once been true of her, she knew that. Was it possible she was still sacrificing happiness in exchange for safety and security?

"Tell me what you dislike most about the relationship," Dr. Carpenter said.

Cindy had had no intention of sharing any such thing with him, but even as she was reeling from the implications of what he'd already said she found herself answering.

"He's not as physically affectionate as I'd like him to be."

"Just sometimes or all the time?"

"Most of the time."

"Why?"

She took a deep breath. "We come from two different religious backgrounds and long story short we haven't been publically open about our relationship."

"So, no kissing in front of other people because then they'd find out?"

"We can't even hold hands."

"That must be very frustrating."

"It is. It's like sometimes it doesn't even feel like we're dating."

"What about when you're alone?"

"He's always very restrained."

"Why do you think that is?"

"I wish I knew," Cindy said.

"Have you told him you wish him to be more demonstrative?"

"Yes."

"Have you really pushed to take your relationship into the open?"

"No."

"Why not?" he asked.

"Because..." she drifted off, struggling to understand her own motivations in that regard. "Because I respect his wishes and I understand where he's coming from."

"You're lying to yourself right now, Cindy," Dr. Carpenter said very quietly.

"Because I'm afraid if I make it an issue, I'll lose him," she said, heart beginning to pound.

"And as much as you're craving a relationship you don't have to hide, as much as you're craving being able to kiss him whenever you want, it's not worth risking the feeling of safety that he gives you."

"Oh my gosh," Cindy said. She felt like she had just been turned inside out.

"It's okay," Dr. Carpenter said, his voice soft, gentle even. "We are raised believing that we are complex creatures. It can be a shock when we realize the truth."

"What truth is that?" Cindy asked, feeling tears begin to slide down her cheeks.

"That we are driven by only one or two things and that we will sacrifice everything else in our lives to obtain those one or two things. For you it's safety. You'll sacrifice a normal, healthy relationship for it, and I suspect that's just the tip of the iceberg. I think you've sacrificed everything your life could have been on that altar. Now that you realize it, you have a choice. Do you continue to sacrifice? Or do you cast down the false idol that you have been worshipping and realize that safety in itself is an illusion. No one can promise it to you anymore than anyone can actually give it to you."

They sat for a minute in complete silence while Cindy reflected on what he'd just said. Tears continued to stream down her face. There was so much to process, to think about, and it scared her.

"There's a chair outside and some bottled water. There's apple juice, too, which is good for stress. You can go ahead and send him in," Dr. Carpenter finally said.

Feeling emotionally raw and physically numb Cindy rose and opened the door. Jeremiah stood up from the chair outside and started toward her.

"What happened?" he asked, and she could see the cracks in the mask of neutrality he was trying to wear. She could feel his concern for her. For her well-being. For her safety.

She started to cry harder. "It's your turn," was all she managed to get out.

He stood there, looking like he wanted to object, but he finally went inside, closing the door.

Cindy got a bottle of apple juice out of the mini fridge and sat down in the chair Jeremiah had vacated. Even as she tried to pull herself together she found herself wondering what Jeremiah and Dr. Carpenter were saying.

14

Jeremiah sat on the couch, body language carefully neutral. Dr. Carpenter was staring at him intently, but Jeremiah had withstood interrogation by psychologists before and he was determined to give the man nothing he didn't need to. He had made Cindy cry and that wasn't a good thing. He knew he had to at least talk to the man and work to keep their cover intact, but he didn't have to let the psychologist walk around in his head.

"You love her?" Dr. Carpenter asked.

"Yes."

"Why?"

"She's special."

"Undoubtedly, but which of her attributes do you find special?"

"She is open-hearted, generous, loving, kind, compassionate, funny."

"In other words, everything you are not."

The psychologist was almost certainly taking a stab in the dark.

"I love that she's curious and tenacious. Her faith is beautiful as is she."

"You have her on a pedestal."

"That's where she belongs," Jeremiah said.

"She's unattainable."

"No."

"But you think she should be," Dr. Carpenter said. "You are beneath her, this is how you feel, what you believe. She deserves better than you."

"She deserves better than anyone," Jeremiah said.

"Which is why she's untouchable, not to be sullied. Because you cherish her innocence and you would do anything to protect it. And because you believe that she should leave you and one day she will figure that out, too."

Jeremiah struggled not to give any reaction. The man was perceptive. Still he could have inferred a lot of this from things Cindy might have said to him.

"So, tell me, what is it you haven't forgiven yourself for that you have not allowed yourself to find happiness with this woman you love?"

"Nothing."

The man narrowed his eyes. "Lying helps none of us at this point. I can only help if you are willing to be honest with yourself, and with me, and with her."

Jeremiah took a deep breath. "Everything."

"Now that is the truth," Dr. Carpenter said, leaning forward. "And yet she has forgiven you?"

"Yes."

"And you believe it was wrong of her to do so?"

"Naïve."

"And yet that is one of her qualities that you prize most."

"There is a difference between innocent and naïve."

"Indeed there is," Dr. Carpenter said, sitting back in his chair.

"You've been watching us, observing us since we arrived," Jeremiah accused.

"I watched how you interacted with each other and the others at the meet-and-greet the first night. I observe how you are at mealtimes. I've even observed some of the morning session. I am not just observing you, but everyone."

"Because how else are you supposed to do your job when you get an hour with two people to try and fix what is wrong with them?"

Dr. Carpenter smiled. "I knew I didn't like you. You're too perceptive and you wear a mask as though it were your own skin. In my experience there are only a couple of types of men who are as you are and none of them are good."

"Is that a fact," Jeremiah said, smiling as well. He refused to let his mask slip, though, and give the doctor a good look at what really lurked beneath.

"Yes. I think you love this woman because she forgives you your sins and sees what you can be and her vision of you both excites and frightens you. She makes you want to strive to be the man who could be worthy of her while at the same time reinforcing the belief that you could never be a man worthy of her."

"Why did you make her cry?" Jeremiah asked.

"That was not my doing. Her tears came from inside her, from knowledge that she was unwilling to embrace, but now understands to be true."

Jeremiah was getting angry. "If you turned her against me-"

"I have done no such thing. The only one who can turn her against you is you, and I believe you've been doing an excellent job of just that."

"What do you mean?" Jeremiah asked.

"Tell her it's time for her to come in now."

Jeremiah struggled to get his emotions under control as he went to the door to get Cindy. He had been questioned, interrogated, tortured by some of the most gifted and devious people on the planet. Dr. Carpenter was one of the best he'd ever encountered. The man had almost a sixth sense for honing in on patterns of behavior, verbal and nonverbal cues, all to get to the core of a person's being. He was brilliant. The question was, what was someone with his skills doing in a place like this? He probably could pull in ten times the money working somewhere with a higher profile. It made Jeremiah wonder what skeletons were hiding in the doctor's closet that he'd put himself wholly in hiding.

Cindy stood up when he opened the door. She had a bottle of apple juice clutched in her hands that was half-empty. At least her tears had stopped. She came inside and went to sit on the couch without saying a word. Jeremiah closed the door and then went and sat beside her.

The psychologist studied them both for a minute. Finally he leaned forward in his chair.

"Kiss," he instructed.

"Excuse me?" Jeremiah asked.

Cindy looked up, clearly startled.

"You heard me. Kiss right now."

Jeremiah was about to protest, but Cindy turned to him, leaned in, and kissed him on the lips. She pulled back quickly as her cheeks turned pink.

"Okay, let's try that again. Jeremiah, since you didn't participate the first time, this time you have to kiss her. Cindy, feel free not to reciprocate just so he knows how that felt for you."

155

Jeremiah didn't know what the point of this exercise was, but he told himself to just cool down and do as the man wanted.

"Kiss. Anytime now."

Jeremiah leaned over and kissed Cindy. She didn't kiss back. Instead of ending it, he found himself kissing her more, trying to entice her to return the kiss. For just a moment he felt himself start to panic.

He forced himself to break the contact. Cindy was just doing as instructed, her lack of response had nothing to do with her not wanting to kiss him.

"Didn't feel good, did it?" Dr. Carpenter asked.

"What's the point of all this?" Jeremiah asked.

"Physical expressions of love and intimacy should be natural and mutual, not forced, and not withheld. The two of you are having problems making those expressions in a natural way. Frankly, I think that's because you don't engage in them enough. Holding hands, kissing, these should become second nature, almost habit to you. For the rest of the retreat, any time you see another couple hold hands, I want you to do the same. If another couple kisses, so should you."

"Okay," Cindy said quickly.

"This, of course, is only addressing a symptom of the problem. In order to fix things, we have to address the problem itself."

"And what would that be?" Jeremiah asked.

"Almost all of human behavior can be attributed to two driving instincts. They are: what a person wants most and what a person fears most. If you know these two things about a person you can predict what they will do more than ninety percent of the time. Here, the two of you are sharing the same basic fear. It comes from a different place for both of you, but the fundamental fear itself is the same. You are afraid of losing each other."

Jeremiah glanced at Cindy who was looking back at him. She looked like she was in even more distress than he was.

Dr. Carpenter continued. "For Cindy, because she's afraid of losing you, she's willing to accept a relationship that is merely a shadow of what a real relationship should be without objecting too strenuously. For Jeremiah, because he's afraid that you're too good for him and will ultimately leave, he has a hard time touching you because he doesn't want to taint you or have you recognize that you don't actually want his kisses or him."

Jeremiah wanted to say something, but he couldn't. To have a stranger lay it all out like that, and with such devastating accuracy, was tough to take.

"Okay, you two have a lot to think about, talk about, and *do*. Over the next couple of days I want to see more PDA out of the two of you than out of all the other couples here combined, is that clear?"

"What's PDA?" Jeremiah asked.

"Public Displays of Affection," Cindy said quietly.

"Is that clear?" Dr. Carpenter repeated, raising his voice.

Jeremiah turned and kissed Cindy. This time she kissed him back. As they stood up he locked eyes with the psychologist. "Clear."

They made it back to their room, but there was no time to discuss anything as they quickly got ready for dinner and prepared to help Tristan and Beth discover the fake journal.

"It looks like they're still in their bungalow," Jeremiah remarked. "Are you ready to do this?"

Cindy nodded. In between yoga and their small group session Jeremiah had actually been able to race back, grab the journal, break into Tristan and Beth's bungalow to hide it, and make it back. It had been a last minute change in plans but she was grateful that the book was already in place and that she wasn't going to have to carry it in surreptitiously as originally planned. Thanks to Dr. Carpenter, her mind was far too preoccupied to have been able to pull that off right then.

She was wearing her new red dress and Jeremiah had already complimented her three times on it. They approached Tristan and Beth's door and knocked.

Tristan opened the door. "Hey, what are you guys doing here?" he asked, clearly surprised.

"I was needing a little wardrobe assistance and I was hoping Beth could help," Cindy said.

"Sure come on in," Tristan said, standing aside to give them room to enter. "Beth, Cindy and Jeremiah are here. She needs your help."

Beth came out of the bathroom, futzing with her left earring. "What's going on?" she asked.

Cindy stepped forward. "I need help pinning the back of my dress so nothing shows," she said.

"Oh, sure, come back here and we'll take care of it," Beth said.

Cindy nodded and put her purse down on the dresser. She had a couple of safety pins in her other hand and she followed Beth into the bathroom.

"I thought I packed the bra that would work with this dress, but apparently not," Cindy said as she handed the safety pins to Beth.

"It happens. We'll get you fixed up, though. Turn around."

Cindy did as she was told and a minute later Beth had pinned her straps in the back so that they weren't showing.

"There, perfect!" Beth said.

"Thank you so much."

"I'm glad to help. Now we're both finished up, we can all walk over for dinner."

"That sounds good," Cindy said.

She walked over to the dresser, went to pick up her purse, and instead knocked it onto the ground. When she had set it down she had purposely left it unzipped so that its contents spilled on the floor.

"Dang it," Cindy said as she bent down to start scooping things up.

Beth crouched down next to her and together they scooped Cindy's stuff back into her purse. Beth's eyes finally focused on the journal which was just behind the dresser as though it had fallen down behind, but with the slightest edge peeking out.

"Is this yours?" Beth asked, reaching to pull the journal free.

"No, it's not," Cindy said. "Isn't it yours?"

"No." Beth flipped it open. "There's a name inside. It belongs to a Malcolm Griffith. Must have been one of the previous guests. It fell down behind here and he didn't see it when he checked out."

"I'm sure if you drop it at the front desk they can mail it home to him."

"Yeah, good idea. Something like this I'm sure he'll be eager to get it back." Beth flipped a couple more pages. "Look, an envelope addressed to a woman with the same last name. I bet that this is his home address and she's his wife."

"You're probably right."

For one heart-stopping moment Cindy thought that Beth was going to open the envelope. She heaved a sigh of relief when Beth tucked it back in the book.

"I'll drop it off at the front desk and we can go in and have dinner," Beth said.

The four of them left the bungalow. Cindy grabbed Jeremiah's hand and he squeezed hers so tightly it almost hurt. So far, so good.

They made it into the main building and Beth moved right over to the front desk where a woman was talking on the phone and typing away on the computer keyboard. She hung up the phone as Beth approached.

"Can I help you?"

"Yes, we found this in our room. We think it belonged to a former guest, a Malcolm Griffith. I just wanted to turn it in so hopefully you can get it back to him."

"Oh, thank you," the woman said, clearly startled as she took the journal from Beth.

"No problem," Beth said as she turned and headed into the dining room with Tristan.

"We'll be right in," Cindy said, making a pretext of searching for something in her purse while Jeremiah kept an eye on the woman with the journal.

"What are you looking for?" Jeremiah asked.

"My aspirin bottle. I thought for sure I'd put it in here," Cindy said, speaking slowly and stalling for time.

She casually glanced over at the woman behind the desk. She was wearing a deer in the headlights sort of expression and she was still holding the book.

"Maybe you left it back in the room," Jeremiah said.

"I guess I must have."

"Would you like me to run back and get it for you?"

"That would be wonderful, thank you."

"Okay, I'll be back in a couple of minutes," he said.

"I'll see you in the dining room," Cindy affirmed.

Jeremiah left out the doors they had come in. Cindy lingered for another moment before proceeding inside into the dining room. She sat down at their table. "Jeremiah had to run back to the room to get some aspirin for me," she said.

"Are you feeling alright?" Dorothea asked.

"I'll be fine," Cindy said with a smile.

Outside the glass doors Jeremiah had angled himself in position so he could watch the woman with the book. He had his cell phone pressed to his ear and occasionally nodded or said something to keep up the illusion that he was on a phone call. A couple more people drifted in, not even giving him a second glance.

The woman behind the desk was growing increasingly agitated. She tried to put the journal away in a cabinet beneath the counter and then almost as quickly as she shoved it there she pulled it back out.

Finally the lobby was clear with everyone who had walked in now in the dining room. She pulled a cell phone out of her pocket and called someone. Fortunately he was close enough to be able to read her lips.

It's me. We've got a problem.

There was a pause and then she continued.

The couple in bungalow nine just brought in a journal they found in their room that belonged to Malcolm Griffith.

Another pause.

No, I don't know what's in it!

As she listened she was growing even more agitated, her free hand clenching into a fist.

No, I don't know where they found it. I don't think they read it, but I don't know. What do you want me to do?

After a couple seconds she started shaking her head violently.

No, I'm not going there by myself.

Another pause.

Okay, we can meet up tonight at the storeroom after everyone's asleep and we'll both go. When? Fine. I gotta go.

She ended the call. She glanced around anxiously and then headed for the door with the book held tight. Jeremiah casually turned his back to the door.

"Uh huh, yeah, sure," he said into the phone as she hurried out of the building and headed away.

He briefly considered following her, but that seemed like taking an unnecessary chance. After all, he knew where she'd be later that night.

"Bye," he said to his imaginary caller before shoving his phone into his pocket. He pulled a small bottle of aspirin out of the other one and then headed inside and made his way to their table.

"Sorry, it took me a couple of minutes to find it," he said, handing Cindy the bottle of aspirin.

"Well, at least you found it," she said, taking one and putting the bottle into her purse.

"Yes, it's all good," he said with a meaningful glance as he took his seat.

"We were just talking about how much fun we have every year doing the horseback ride," Flynn said.

"Yes, you simply must do it," Dorothea chimed in. "The scenery is beautiful and it's you, the horse, and nature in all its beauty. It really gives a person time to think."

Jeremiah smiled. "I'm pretty sure we're not going to get Cindy on a horse. Her last experience with that was...less than pleasant."

Cindy rolled her eyes. "That would be putting it mildly."

"What happened? You weren't hurt were you?" Beth asked.

"No, but I was certainly terrified."

"Given how many times the two of you have been here, you must know all the ins and outs of this place," Jeremiah said, addressing Flynn and Dorothea.

"Oh, we do," the older lady beamed.

"Anything you could want to know we could probably answer just as well, if not better than, most of the staff," Flynn agreed.

"That's quite a feat. You must know all the staff pretty well at this point, too," Jeremiah said.

"Some better than others," Flynn admitted. "There are a few new faces this year so it will be interesting to get to know them as well."

"Like who?" Cindy asked.

"Summer, the yoga instructor is new," Dorothea said.

"Lancaster is new, too. I'm not sure what it is he does," Flynn added.

"He's a masseuse," Beth said.

"Only two new people in the last year? That's still pretty impressive," Jeremiah said.

"Yeah, it must be a good place to work," Cindy said.

"It seems to be. I do miss the old yoga instructor. I wish I knew why she quit," Dorothea said. "Oh well, hopefully she's where she wants to be doing what she loves."

"When did she leave?" Cindy asked.

"Arnold said she'd been gone about six months," Flynn said. "It is a shame. She was quite good, although Summer seems nice."

Cindy knew it was good information that they were gathering, but she was restless. She kept wanting to be out, doing. It was driving her crazy that she couldn't ask Jeremiah what he had found out. She was so keyed up she could barely touch her food.

Later at the last session of the evening she found she couldn't even begin to concentrate. When they were finally dismissed she grabbed Jeremiah's hand and half-ran, half-walked back to their bungalow. When they got inside she turned to him eagerly.

"Well?"

"Well, she most certainly knew who Malcolm was and the journal freaked her out," he told her.

"I could tell that much from her reaction when Beth gave it to her. What *else* did you learn?"

"She called someone to let them know about it. Her accomplice asked her to do something with the journal, but she refused to go wherever it was by herself. So they're meeting tonight at the storeroom and going together."

"When?"

"I don't know, but it's supposed to be late after everyone's asleep."

"Do you think she was the woman you saw last night?"

"I have no way of knowing at this point, but I hope so. It would certainly make things easier, less complicated."

"I vote for that."

"One way or another we'll know more tonight."

"So, what is the gameplan?"

"Get to the storage room before them and hide ourselves really well. Then follow if we can."

She smiled, liking that he was including her in that plan. There was no way she was going to want to stay behind again, especially if there was even the slimmest chance of still saving Malcolm.

They both changed into all black clothes. The bathing suit ruse could only really work once and certainly not if they were found in a building that was for staff only. At last they set out, Jeremiah holding her hand as they walked softly past the rows of bungalows. A couple still had lights on, but most did not.

Jeremiah was like a big cat on the prowl, hunting his prey. She watched his every movement, trusting him implicitly. At last they arrived at their destination and he inspected it for a good minute before easing the door open and letting them both inside.

Once in the building they moved swiftly. On the right hand wall was a massive metal shelving unit anchored to the wall. Jeremiah quickly moved a few things and then helped her slide onto the bottom shelf. He then maneuvered various cans and jars in front of her so that her entire body was obscured. He left her a small slit that she could look out through.

She felt a little claustrophobic. It would not be a space she could slip out of easily or quietly. If she was caught there'd be no way she could escape. But that was what Jeremiah was for. And she had to admit that it was an ingenious hiding place. She never would have guessed a person would fit on the shelf along with other goods.

She took several deep breaths and told herself that the likelihood of her being found was pretty much zero unless something truly unfortunate happened like she sneezed.

Her arms were pinned to her sides and she couldn't move. She was scarcely daring to breathe. She didn't know where Jeremiah was hiding. All she knew was that she couldn't see him. She had another tiny moment of panic, but kept breathing evenly and deeply until the feelings subsided. Jeremiah would be close by, watching over her, protecting her, just as he always did. That was one of the things that she could count on for an absolute certainty. As long as he had breath in his body he would always come for her, always save her. The thought warmed her through and through until she had nearly forgotten that she was trapped in a confined space with no room to move.

Just as she really started to relax and settle down to wait there was a loud crashing sound as the door to the building was thrown open.

15

Cindy tried to keep her breathing calm and even as someone walked into the building carrying a flashlight. It sounded loud to her ears, but then again, she could swear she also heard her heart beating. She knew that she just needed to keep herself calm and it would be okay.

She tried to focus instead on the person who had entered the building. Unfortunately from the angle she was at, and the way they were moving the flashlight, she couldn't get a good look at who it might be. Hopefully Jeremiah had a better vantage point than she did.

Whoever it was seemed to settle in to wait. Five minutes later the door opened again, but quietly this time.

"You're late," a woman's voice said, sounding agitated. Cindy thought it might be the woman Beth had handed the journal to.

"Keep your voice down. Show me the journal," the newcomer said in a husky whisper. Cindy couldn't even tell if it was a man or a woman speaking. She could see their legs, but whoever it was had on jeans and tennis shoes.

"Look," the woman from the lobby said.

"How did they miss this?"

Cindy felt herself go cold. *They.* As in more than one and not the two people already in this room. That meant at least four people were involved.

"There's a letter in there the guy wrote to his wife. I think he knew something was going to happen to him."

"That's impossible."

"Oh, yeah? Then why's he telling her where he hid money and a diamond? And get this, they were with him. Did they even open his briefcase?"

"I don't know."

"If they didn't they missed it and if they did then they're holding out on us."

The second speaker swore. Paused, then swore again.

"What are we going to do?"

"This changes everything. We were just going to bury this tonight, but now we're going to have to dig up the body."

Cindy felt an icy cold spreading through her. Malcolm was dead. Something inside her had thought so all along, but it was awful to actually have it confirmed. She felt so sorry for his wife, his friends. Mark's captain was going to be devastated.

"I don't want to dig up a body," the girl from the lobby whined.

"I need time to think. This changes nothing in the current plan. We'll talk later. Wait two minutes and then leave."

Cindy tensed, expecting Jeremiah to make a move at any moment. Nothing happened, though, and the unknown speaker turned and left, closing the door softly behind them. And the woman from the lobby waited barely a minute before scurrying out.

Seconds later Jeremiah was clearing a path to help Cindy out from her hiding spot.

"Did you see who the second person was?" she asked.

"I think it was Summer, the yoga instructor, but I couldn't get a clear enough look at her face to swear to it."

"Malcolm is dead."

"Yes, he is," Jeremiah confirmed.

"Why didn't we do something? Grab them and call Mark or something?" Cindy asked, feeling a bit sick to her stomach over the whole thing. "Are we calling him now so he can come arrest them?"

"No."

"Why not? We heard them say he was dead."

"But we didn't hear them confess to killing him. Even if we had, that wouldn't be enough."

"What? How?

"We're on thin ice out here. We're not going to be able to bring in police without proof that there's been a murder. We have none. There's no body, no motive, we don't even know who killed him or when or where or even how. We have absolutely nothing. At this point it's our word versus theirs that he was ever even here at the resort."

Cindy could feel anger and frustration burning within her. As she was able to stand up and move away from her hiding spot she clenched her hands into fists so hard that her fingernails began to cut into her palms.

"They might have erased him from the reservation system on the computer, but there's the spreadsheets with his name on them."

"And they can say that he was a no show or canceled his reservation so they took him out of the system but never got him removed from the activities roster. They can even say that he was here but left and their system is just glitchy sometimes."

"But the entire staff would have known he was here."

"And how many of them are in on it? And if there are any who aren't, how many of them are going to risk their jobs contradicting the others?"

"Mark should start tracking down the other guests who were here, someone has to remember him."

"And in order to figure out who those other guests were, he would need to get at the resort's records which they are not going to give up willingly, and he is almost certainly not going to be able to get a warrant for."

"They're going to win," Cindy said, feeling numbness creeping over her at the realization. "The bad guys are going to win."

Jeremiah wrapped his hands around her shoulders. "I promise you they're not."

"How do you know that?" she asked.

"Because I know us. We don't give up, we don't back down, and we always find the killer. We can do this."

"Okay," she said, taking a deep breath.

"Good."

"Do you think Summer, or whoever that was, will try to bury the journal tonight? Should we be following her?"

"No," Jeremiah said. "I'm pretty sure that she does want to think it over. She may even want to show it to some of the others or try to use it to gain some leverage over them. Either way I don't see her destroying it tonight and she certainly won't be digging up a grave on her own."

"So, you think it's safe to get some sleep?"

"Not only safe, but a very wise idea. Things are going to get crazy around here. We've knocked down the hornets' nest and now we have to see which way we're going to need to run."

171

A terrible new thought occurred to her. "You don't think they'll hurt Tristan or Beth, do you?"

He shook his head slowly. "Not unless they suspect that they're actually here trying to figure out what happened to Malcolm. As long as they believe that Beth and Tristan finding that journal was purely by chance they should be alright."

"If we have to use someone else to cast suspicion away from us again, let's use a different couple, preferably one we don't like as much," Cindy said.

"Agreed. Now let's get out of here and back to our room so we can get some sleep and be ready for whatever happens tomorrow."

"Okay."

Jeremiah took her hand and led her silently out of the building. Even as she was trying to tiptoe quietly past the first bungalows on their way back to their own she was shocked at how silently Jeremiah could move. There wasn't a footstep, not a whisper of fabric, nothing. Almost as though he wasn't even there. And she might have started to doubt that he was but for the warmth of his hand around hers.

As for her, every footfall sounded like a gunshot ringing out and echoing round and round. The more quietly she tried to step the louder it seemed to get. Maybe it was just her imagination or the fact that she was revved up and probably being hyper-sensitive to sounds.

She was sure that whoever was doing security rounds was going to hear her and come investigating. She kept trying to find a plausible excuse for why they were out late this time and wearing all black to boot.

It was with a sigh of relief that she entered their bungalow and Jeremiah locked the door behind them. She was exhausted, mentally and physically. She needed sleep right now in a bad way. She kept telling herself that sleep would make everything better, but she wasn't buying it.

"You okay?" Jeremiah asked.

She shook her head as she turned to face him.

"What do you need?" he asked.

"Hold me," she said.

He stepped forward and wrapped his arms around her. Tears started to slide down her cheeks.

"This is stupid. I'm crying and I didn't even know the guy."

"You had a great deal of compassion for him, particularly when you thought he might have been kidnapped as you once were. Plus, you're having a lot of empathy for those back home who've been so worried."

She nodded. It all made sense. She shuddered, though, as she realized what they had to do next.

"We need to call Mark so he can let Malcolm's widow know. She's waited long enough for an answer. It will destroy her, but then the waiting will be over and the healing can begin."

"You're right. We'll call him in a couple of minutes," Jeremiah said, kissing the top of her head.

"Okay," she said, holding tight to him as the tears continued to flow.

So many dark thoughts crowded her mind and she tried to push them away. Failing at it, she prayed for help. Thinking of Malcolm's widow kept causing her to relive those hours when she'd thought Jeremiah was dead. It also reminded her that someday he truly would be and that she would lose him forever.

"We'll catch the ones responsible for this. All of them," he said. "They won't get to hurt anyone else ever again."

Mark had been back in bed after a double diaper changing for all of five minutes when his phone rang. He briefly considered throwing it against the wall in the hopes that it would stop and he wouldn't have to deal with whoever was calling.

With a frustrated grunt he sat up, grabbed the phone, and moved into the hallway as he answered.

"Hello?"

"It's Jeremiah."

"Do you have something?" he asked, coming a little more awake.

"News, and it's bad."

"He's dead, isn't he?" Mark asked.

"Yes."

"Dang it. Did you find the body?"

"No, we're working on that. We do know that he was killed, though."

"You got anything I could build a real case on?" Mark asked.

"Not yet, but we're not going to let these people get away with it."

"People, as in more than one?"

"At least four from what we can tell. And whatever their game is, it appears that murder is not the end goal but an accident. Whatever they've been doing it sounds like they've been doing it for a while and something went wrong with Malcolm."

"Okay, what do you need from me?

"I don't know yet, but as soon as I do believe me I'll be calling."

Mark hung up the phone and stood for a moment, gathering himself before calling the captain. It was always bad enough delivering this kind of news to strangers but it was nearly impossible to deliver it to people he knew. He took a deep breath and made the call.

Jeremiah got ready for bed. It had been a long, frustrating night. Their ruse had worked, but Cindy was taking the news that Malcolm was already dead pretty hard. What was worse was he didn't know how to help her.

When he'd finished up in the bathroom he turned off the light and walked into the bedroom. She was sitting on the edge of her bed, frowning as though deep in thought. She was wearing pajamas with cavorting cats on them and she looked adorable.

"You okay?"

"Yeah, just thinking," she said. She looked up at him and tried to force a smile. "So, what's on the schedule for tomorrow?"

He walked over to the table and picked up the papers they'd received upon check-in. "Let's see, tomorrow we have the same thing in the morning: breakfast, group session, and lunch. Then in the afternoon we have some free time, then ballroom dancing followed by a small group session with Jasmine."

"The hugger?" Cindy asked.

"That would be the one."

"And the two women said they were going ahead with their plans as scheduled. So, we need to still be watching and to figure out what they're trying to pull people into."

"Exactly."

Cindy looked like she wanted to say something else, but she just shook her head. "It's going to be a busy day, we should probably get some sleep."

"Are you sure you're okay?" he asked her.

"I will be," she said.

He decided not to push. A lot had happened in the last few hours that had shaken them both. She would share when she was ready. He turned off the lights around the room and then climbed into his bed. After a minute Cindy clicked off the lamp on the nightstand, plunging the room into darkness. He could hear her as she laid down, and then she messed with her covers for a few minutes.

It was going to be an interesting day. Now that they knew that Malcolm was dead they could pursue answers a little more aggressively without worrying that he had only been kidnapped and might get hurt.

He understood why Cindy was so frustrated. Sometimes justice was a lot harder to obtain than it should be. He really wished there was more they could do and faster.

If Malcolm was an outlier then it was a good guess that whatever they were doing with these people, killing them wasn't part of the plan. And yet even though they were on tribal land it wasn't like the people at the resort were doing something that would cause a hue and cry from their former clientele. Which meant that whatever it was, they were getting people to do voluntarily. They seemed to be targeting people with money, or at least people they thought had money.

It couldn't be something like an investment scheme, because how would something like that have gone so badly with Malcolm so quickly? There had to be others out there who had been approached, participated in whatever this was. If only they could find and talk to them.

Mark.

Mark was on the outside and he could do that. Jeremiah had been thinking about the fact that no judge was going to issue a warrant for him to obtain the resort's client list.

But they didn't necessarily need former clients who could testify. They just needed one to clue them in as to what was going on.

Cindy's breathing had evened out and was gentle and rhythmic. She had finally fallen asleep which was good. She needed it. As quietly as he could he got up, grabbed the clothes he'd been wearing earlier, and went into the bathroom to change.

When he emerged Cindy was still asleep. He slipped on his shoes, put his cell in his one pocket and his keycard and a blank piece of resort stationery in his other. After only a moment's hesitation he also grabbed the Minox camera he had brought on the trip just in case. He slid it into his shirt pocket then he let himself out as quietly as he could.

He moved swiftly to the main building, easily avoiding the couple of surveillance cameras that he knew about. He kept his eyes and ears on alert, looking and listening for any sign of a staff member patrolling the grounds. Of course, at this time of night anyone else who was walking around would be up to something.

Just like he was.

He made it to the main building and slipped inside. He made a beeline for the computer and in seconds he had the reservation system up and running. After looking around the system for a minute, he was able to find a way to pull together a spreadsheet of all clients from a certain time frame. He created one for everyone who had been at the resort in the last six weeks.

There were far too many names to write down and he had no way of telling who might have been a potential target. He slid the Minox out of his pocket. The camera was tiny, and its type was commonly referred to as the spy camera with good reason. And even in the age of smartphones it was an important tool because of the quality of the pictures it took, even at extreme close range, and because it was a fraction the size of a smartphone.

Less than a minute later he'd taken pictures of everything he needed. He shut the program down. He started to slip the camera back into his pocket, but he paused. Something deep down urged him not to.

Whenever he had that prompting, he had learned to obey. He had often thought it was G-d warning him. Whether it was or not he knew that it had never steered him wrong.

He bent down and slipped the camera into his shoe. It was a tight fit, but at least it would be concealed. Finished, he rose and walked around the other side of the counter. He made it into the center of the room and paused. He'd heard something. He knew he had. From where he was standing he could see into the dining room and there was no one there. A door on the far side led to a kitchen area. Both the gym and the yoga studio were dark and deserted looking.

The hair rose on the back of his neck and in that moment he knew that he was about to get caught.

16

Jeremiah weighed his options. There were multiple places he could hide, but without knowing where someone would be coming from and where they would be going to it made it difficult. The multitude of windows in the building also allowed it to be flooded by a lot of moonlight making dark shadowy places few and far between.

He heard a scraping sound. It was possible that whoever was coming his way was trying to be stealthy as well. Either way there was one option that would serve him best at this point. He quickly rolled his long sleeves up to his elbows to de-emphasize the fact that he was wearing all black.

"Hello? Is anyone around? I need some help," Jeremiah called.

There was a moment of silence in which the other person was clearly trying to decide how to respond.

"Anyone?" Jeremiah called one last time. If there continued to be no answer he would turn and walk out the door.

A section of the wall behind the front desk opened, a door that he hadn't noticed before. A dim light was burning in the room beyond which was likely a back office area.

Arnold stepped through, not bothering to hide the scowl on his face.

"What are you doing up?" he asked bluntly.

Jeremiah pulled his keycard out of his pocket. "My card demagnetized and I need help getting it fixed. I must have put it too close to my phone without thinking."

Simple and to the point. People who weren't feeling guilty or like they had anything to hide were more likely to make simple, direct requests.

"Why couldn't you wait until morning?" Arnold asked.

"Because I need it to get back in my room now," Jeremiah said, acting like it was the most natural answer in the world and like he was surprised that he would even have to say it out loud.

"And why are you not in your room at this time of the night?"

"Oh, well, Cindy and I had a...bit of a disagreement. I couldn't sleep so I decided to take a walk, clear my head, you know, before I said anything stupid."

"And she wouldn't let you in when you came back to the room?"

"She sleeps like the dead. I don't how she does it, but she does. I knocked for five minutes when I realized my card wasn't working. I didn't want to kick the door or shout because I didn't want to wake anyone else up. So, I figured there must be someone out here at night in case of emergencies and things. It was all dark, though, so I didn't think there was. I have to admit I'm relieved to see you."

He could tell from the look on Arnold's face that the man was still wavering slightly in his suspicion. Jeremiah stepped forward and handed him his keycard. "Bungalow fourteen," he said with a smile. "And, I'd appreciate it if you didn't tell the other staff members we were fighting. It's embarrassing."

"It could be worse," Arnold commented as he took the keycard.

"Yeah, she could have told me I could go sleep on the yoga mats or something," Jeremiah said, giving a nervous edge to his voice to give the impression that Cindy had indeed actually said that.

Arnold visibly relaxed. "Here, empty your pockets on the counter."

"Why?"

"I just want to see what you're carrying. Sometimes people don't realize exactly what is demagnetizing their cards. I've helped more than one person discover the true culprit so it would stop happening to them."

While Jeremiah did not doubt that what the man said was true, he also knew Arnold wanted to get a look at what he had on him, just in case. Despite the tightness in his shoe and the discomfort to his instep, Jeremiah was grateful that the camera was safely stowed there.

"Okay, but I'm pretty sure it's my phone," he said, pulling first the phone then the blank piece of paper out of his pockets.

"Anything in your shirt pocket?" Arnold asked, eyeing it.

"No," Jeremiah said, pulling it out slightly.

"You don't have your wallet with you," Arnold noted.

"I didn't need it. I wasn't going anywhere and there was nothing to buy. Although, if you'd like a little feedback, you could really do with a soda vending machine. I could kill for a Coca Cola right about now."

"Yes, I bet you could. I was going to check your wallet. Some have magnetic clasps on them. Also, if you stack your cards so that the magnetic strips are touching each other that can cause problems."

"I never knew that, thanks for the tip," Jeremiah said. He put the phone and the piece of paper back in his pocket.

Arnold gave him a strained smile. "It'll take me a couple of minutes to get into the system so I can reset your card."

"I understand. At night at my work we turn off all the computers, too. Saves electricity and wear and tear."

And by indicating that he thought Arnold's computer was turned off, he implied that he had not been behind the counter to see that it wasn't.

"Do you want to talk about what the fight was over?" Arnold asked.

Jeremiah hesitated before saying, "I do, but I shouldn't. I'd have to betray her trust to do so and I'm not quite ready to do that just yet."

Again an implication, this time that he might be enticed into doing so. They seemed to be targeting couples where the partners could be easily separated from each other. He wanted to plant the seeds that he and Cindy might not be glued at the hip in case Arnold was in on whatever was going on.

"If you change your mind, let me know. I'm here to help."

About a minute later Arnold swiped Jeremiah's card and then handed it to him. "Make sure to keep it away from your phone this time."

"I will. Hey, you're the boss, how come you're the one stuck holding down the fort in the middle of the night?"

"Everyone has to pull their weight," Arnold said with a tight smile. "And, as you pointed out, I'm the boss which brings with it a good deal of paperwork that is easiest to deal with when I'm not being disturbed."

"Sorry. Well, have a good rest of your night. I'll see you in the morning," Jeremiah said, turning and heading for the door.

Once outside he moved swiftly. He made it back to the bungalow and quietly let himself inside. Cindy appeared to still be asleep which was lucky for him.

He removed the camera from his shoe and put it on the table. He grabbed some equipment from his bag and minutes later had emailed Mark the images containing the names and contact information of past resort guests. Hopefully he'd be able to get something useful out of it.

He thought about calling Mark to alert him to look for it. It was the middle of the night, though. There was a chance he'd gone back to bed already. A call would surely wake Cindy up, too. Jeremiah settled for sending Mark a text telling him to check his email. That done, he hastily began to get ready for bed a second time.

Mark's phone chimed just as he was drifting off to sleep. He opened one eye and saw that Jeremiah had texted something. Mark picked up the phone. If the rabbi wasn't dead or dying then Mark was going to kill him.

Check your email.

Great, cryptic as usual. Mark dropped the phone back on the nightstand in disgust. No way was he getting up. If it was an emergency Jeremiah would have called. Mark flipped onto his side, fluffed his pillow and closed his eyes.

Unless for some reason he can't call.

He punched his pillow, cursing its sudden lumpiness. That was ridiculous. If he could text he could call. It couldn't be an emergency.

Unless he and Cindy have been pinned down and he couldn't risk revealing their location by talking.

Mark flipped on his other side, punched the pillow again just for good measure. That was ridiculous. They should be safe and secure in their room. No one knew who they were and they hadn't been caught when snooping around earlier.

Unless they went back out to track down a lead.

Mark folded his pillow in half and threw himself on his back, the entire bed shaking with his effort. Still Traci slept on, snoring softly. If it had been an actual emergency Jeremiah would have typed SOS or 911 or something besides instructions regarding email.

Unless someone else was using his phone and they've just sent some sort of ransom demand.

Mark sat straight up and seriously considered whether or not shooting his pillow would help. While he pondered it he told himself that a kidnapper would have just called or sent a video image to the phone.

He fell backward and the pillow slid out from beneath his head and fell down between the mattress and the headboard. He was so tired he might just leave it there.

Unless-

Mark sat up, grabbed the phone and called Jeremiah. When Jeremiah answered, before the rabbi could even finish saying "hello", Mark shouted, "Are you alive or not?"

"Alive," Jeremiah said.

"Wrong answer. You're dead because you won't let me sleep. The email, is it an emergency?"

"It's important, but-"

"Will the world come to an end if I open it in the morning instead of right now?"

"No."

"Good. Is there anything else?"

"No."

"Then goodnight."

Mark ended the call and threw the phone. It hit the floor with a dull thud. He rolled onto his stomach and face-planted on the mattress. He didn't need a pillow or a phone or even the covers Traci was now somehow hogging. He just needed to get some sleep.

Rachel began to cry.

Then Ryan.

Then Mark.

Cindy woke in the morning feeling better, calmer than when she'd gone to bed. She sat up slowly and glanced over at Jeremiah. She was surprised to see that he was still asleep. A quick glance at the clock had her up and on her feet. They were running late.

"Jeremiah, wake up," she said.

He groaned and stirred.

She grabbed her clothes and headed into the bathroom to change. When she emerged a couple of minutes later Jeremiah was still asleep, but his covers were pulled up over him. His bare feet were sticking out the end.

"Jeremiah," she called.

When he didn't answer she reached out and tickled the bottom of his left foot. He moved his foot and slowly pulled the covers down so she could see his face again.

"Get up or I'll tickle both feet," she said.

He opened his eyes and regarded her for a moment. "You do realize... I've killed people for less?" he said, a yawn interrupting him in the middle.

"You do realize we're going to be late?" she countered.

He sat up and swung his legs over the side of the bed. He looked like death warmed over.

"What happened to you last night?" she asked.

"I went back out after you fell asleep."

"You what?" she demanded.

"It occurred to me that I could get Mark a list of resort guests for the last several weeks and he could check them out and see if any of them tells a weird story."

"You should have woken me."

"I wanted you to get your sleep."

"You could have been caught."

"I was caught, but it was fine. I don't think Arnold suspects a thing. If he asks, though, we got in a fight last night."

"What?"

"And you may or may not have suggested that I find a yoga mat to sleep on," Jeremiah added as he grabbed some clothes and headed for the bathroom.

"I think you need to tell me everything that happened."

Cindy quietly fumed as Jeremiah quickly filled her in. She had to grudgingly admit it was probably a good thing she hadn't been with him, though, when he'd been caught. It would have been hard to come up with a good explanation of why they were both running around outside with supposedly demagnetized keycards.

By the time they made it to the dining room about half of the couples had already eaten and left. Breakfast was buffet style so people could eat at their own pace. They found that Dorothea and Flynn were still there, lingering over cups of coffee.

"We were beginning to wonder if you two were going to show up," Flynn said with a grin.

"We overslept," Cindy said.

"Sure you did," Dorothea said with a wink.

Cindy flushed. "We did. I think someone forgot to set an alarm."

"Don't worry, you didn't miss anything exciting so far," the older woman said.

"That's a relief," Cindy said, forcing a smile.

"I'm looking forward to the horseback riding today," Dorothea said with a smile.

"Yes, that's almost always one of our favorite activities, right after the ballroom dancing," Flynn chuckled.

"We have ballroom dancing as our middle session this afternoon," Jeremiah commented.

"You'll have a wonderful time," Dorothea said.

After a couple more minutes Dorothea and Flynn headed out.

Cindy finished shoveling down some scrambled eggs and then drank the rest of her orange juice.

"Ready?" Jeremiah asked as he finished his third cup of coffee.

"As I'll ever be, I guess," she admitted.

"Fair enough."

He stood up and once she had done the same he took her hand. She was getting seriously used to that kind of contact between them, and she was starting to realize that it might be hard to go back to their real lives when this was over.

They didn't have time to head back to their bungalow so they went straight to their morning session.

Mark felt like the walking dead, and he was sure he didn't look much better. He had received the email from Jeremiah with the information about past guests. Sifting through it to find people who were well off was not going to be an easy task. Since this wasn't a traditional case he couldn't just pull people's financial records. As much as his captain wanted Malcolm's killer found, he'd been clear about that this morning.

So, Mark had done the next best thing. He was sitting at the kitchen counter at Geanie and Joseph's, going over the information with Joseph. Most of the names on the list were people who lived within a hundred mile radius or so. For now he wasn't even bothering to look at the few outliers who lived farther away.

Even though Joseph was very down to earth and casual in his attitudes about his own fortune he was proving to be an invaluable asset simply because of the number of people he met through charity functions. In addition, Joseph had his own charity, the day-to-day operations of which were overseen by other people, but he'd been heavily involved in fundraising for it at the beginning and was in a position to know who had money just lying around.

They sipped coffee and made small talk while Joseph went over the names one by one. By the end he had a list of ten people. Of the ten, he had put stars by two of them.

"What do the stars mean?" Mark asked.

"Chester is extremely gullible, so if they're running some sort of scam he would be an easy target."

"Okay, and the other one?"

"Wilson, it's just a hunch actually."

"Tell me."

"Every year he and his wife are huge contributors to this one theater. They're the most loyal of patrons. The annual fundraiser was last weekend. I know that they were in town, and I also know they didn't go. The theater manager also called me two days ago to try and get me to increase the size of our donation. It seems they didn't do quite as well as they normally do."

"So, you think Wilson didn't chip in this year?"

"Yeah."

"Guy could have had an off year last year and couldn't afford it."

"No, Eric was spending it up at a charity auction about a week before he went to this retreat center."

"Interesting."

"I'd say so."

"Maybe I should give Mr. Wilson a call and ask him how he liked his stay," Mark said, pulling his cell phone out and checking the number on the sheet.

Joseph shook his head. "You'll never reach them that way. There's an army of assistants standing between the Wilsons and the public at any given time."

"Then what do you suggest?"

Joseph got up and came back a few moments later with his phone. "Calling Marcia direct." He dialed and then put the phone on speaker so Mark could hear as well.

"Joseph, how are you doing?"

"Good Marcia. You?"

"Not bad. Why are you calling?"

"I was surprised I didn't see you and Eric at the theater last week, just wanted to make sure everyone was okay, no one was sick or anything."

"Oh, no, nothing like that."

"I'm glad to hear it. Say, while I've got you on the phone I've got another question. A friend of mine is thinking about hitting this retreat center out on the reservation. I think Eric's been there or was going there and I wanted to know what he thought of the staff. My friend is pretty particular and he can be a bit of a pain if he doesn't get along with the people."

A torrent of profanity that shocked even Mark came pouring out of the phone's speaker.

17

Mark listened in amazement and Joseph winced as the profanity kept going. Finally Marcia stopped.

"So, the staff aren't so great then?"

"Hah. You know, it's no use keeping it a secret anymore. Eric and I are getting a divorce."

"What? No, I thought you two were doing okay?"

"Yeah, if by okay you mean I cleaned up his messes and covered up his gambling addiction for the past few years. That retreat center was his last shot at redemption. He went there to kick the gambling habit."

"I'm guessing that didn't go so well."

The laughter that followed was harsh. Even Mark cringed. He would not want to be Eric in that divorce. "What do you think of a center treating gambling addicts just two miles away from a casino?"

"I take it he found his way there?"

"You better believe he did. And then he lost everything."

"Everything?"

"Every dime that was liquid."

"I'm so sorry to hear that, Marcia." Joseph said, grimacing as he made eye contact with Mark.

"So, tell your friend to steer clear. I'm pretty sure that someone at that center made it easy for him to escape and land us in this mess."

"I will tell him, thanks for the heads up. And for what it's worth, I'm very sorry."

"Don't be," she said, sounding suddenly quite smug. "I'm the one with the best lawyer."

"Right. Good luck. I'll see you on the other side."

Joseph hung up.

"Well, that was awkward," Joseph said.

"Yes, but your hunch was spot on. You ever think about becoming a cop?"

"No, thank heavens. I respect what you do, so much so that I know not to even attempt it myself."

Mark laughed. "At least we have something to go on now."

"Wilson was there for a different retreat than Malcom was."

"Yeah, but they were both rich and both at a retreat alone. I'm thinking that's not a coincidence. Think I have a shot at talking to Wilson himself?"

"I doubt it. I'll see if I can connect, though. It's easier with Marcia, she and I knew each other when we were kids."

Mark's mind was spinning as he was thinking about what they'd just learned. He felt like he was missing a piece of the puzzle, though, somehow. Enticing someone to go gamble when they were already likely to want to gamble was sleazy, but not exactly illegal. There had to be an angle he was missing.

"So, I hear you and Traci and the kids are going to the Valentine's dinner at the church."

"Yup, and I hear that you and Geanie are not."

"That is correct."

"So, are you whisking her off to dinner in some five star restaurant in Paris?"

"No, no five star restaurants." Joseph said, sipping his coffee.

"A private island somewhere?"

"Nope, no islands, private or otherwise."

"Some elaborate themed dinner locally with choirs waiting to burst into song?"

Joseph chuckled. "No themes, no choirs."

"Okay, I give up then. What are you doing for Valentine's Day?"

"Something incredibly romantic."

"I'm listening," Mark said, thoroughly intrigued now.

"We are unplugging completely, no phones, no computers, we're going to disconnect ourselves one hundred percent."

"And?"

"And we're going to go camping for the weekend."

Mark stared at him in shock. "You are kidding, right?"

"No, what makes you say that?"

"Camping? Really? You have all the money in the world and your idea of a big, romantic weekend is to go camping?"

"Geanie and I all alone with zero distractions, yes it is," Joseph said, a smile on his face.

"You realize this time of the year it's going to be freezing at night?"

"Yes, it is," Joseph said, his smile getting even bigger. "But that's what sleeping bags built for two are for."

"And?"

"And a portable battery operated electric heater or two."

Mark laughed and shook his head. "Well, I hope you have fun."

"How can I not? Oh, and Geanie called before you got here and let me know that we're babysitting the weekend after so that you and Traci can get out of town."

That had been quick. Mark shook his head in amazement. Traci must be needing a break even more than him.

"So, where are you two going to go?"

"I don't know yet, but I know where we're not going."

"Where's that?"

"Camping. Traci would kill me."

After lunch they had a free session before they had to go to the ballroom dance lesson. They headed back to the bungalow where Cindy changed clothes while Jeremiah returned a call from Mark.

"How did Mark sound?" Cindy asked as Jeremiah ended the call.

"Asleep. It sounded like I actually woke him up."

"At lunchtime? He must have been up all night."

"He certainly sounded like it. He did have some information. A man Joseph knows named Eric Wilson was here for the most recent retreat targeted at breaking gambling addictions."

"So, he was a gambler?"

"Apparently. And while he was at the camp he managed to make it over to the casino and lose a small fortune."

"I told you it was weird that they have the retreat at a resort two miles from a casino."

"They probably figure that where there's a casino, there are people addicted to gambling," Jeremiah said.

Cindy rolled her eyes. "Yes, and from that angle it makes perfect sense. We've seen their security around here, though. It wouldn't take that long to walk to the casino and it would just be a couple of minutes by car. So, as long as they left the resort, which would be simple, it would be easy to get to the casino. It's not like they're putting people in more of a lockdown situation. As rehab places go this would have to be one of the worst."

"Agreed. Mark's checking on some other guests and he's getting Malcolm's wife to help him take a closer look at all their accounts, see if there was any unusual activity or anything that would connect to the casino even in a roundabout way."

"I don't understand how any of this leads to people having clandestine meetings in the middle of the night and Malcolm ending up dead."

"Neither do I, yet, but at least it's more than we had yesterday." Jeremiah picked his phone back up off the table and pushed a button.

"Who are you calling?"

"Mark."

Before Cindy could say anything else Jeremiah was talking to the detective. "Something Cindy just said got me thinking. Cars aren't allowed here at the resort, so how did Malcolm get here? Uh huh. Okay, thanks."

Jeremiah hung up and tossed the phone back down. "Well?"

"Malcolm's wife only drives in her neighborhood. He had an arrangement with a local company for discount transportation when he needed it. The driver dropped him off at the resort. He was scheduled to pick him up, but two days before the end of the retreat a message was left canceling his pick up service. His wife initially called the company when he was late getting home and then starting calling the resort."

"So, if he went to the casino he either walked or someone drove him."

"Yes."

"I still just don't see how that all fits," Cindy said, feeling frustrated.

"It wouldn't even have been that questionable. After all, Malcolm wasn't here for the gambling addicts retreat."

"I just wish we could push, put a little pressure on someone to talk."

"Unfortunately we do that and we risk all of them running, or worse," Jeremiah said.

Cindy shivered. What was wrong with her? For some reason she was having a hard time taking the threat seriously which wasn't normal. Maybe it was because she hadn't actually seen a body and without that it was almost as if it was just a story someone else was telling her or wild speculation with no basis in fact.

Or maybe it was the fact that she was so totally consumed with figuring out stuff between her and Jeremiah that it was hard to think about anything else. What was it Mark had said when he dropped them off?

For goodness sake, take the time to figure out what the deal is with you two. It would save us all a lot of grief.

She felt like she had taken that to heart. She had been doing a lot of thinking. Trouble was, it was probably time for a lot of talking and they weren't getting many opportunities when they were alone to discuss something other than solving Malcolm's murder.

She shook her head. Even that sounded cold to her, the way she was thinking about it. *Calm down, you're just winding yourself up.*

She took a deep breath and glanced at the clock. It was time to face the music. Literally.

"We don't really have much occasion to go dancing," Cindy said, cheeks flushing.

Jeremiah couldn't help but smile. Clearly she was more than a little self-conscious about the entire thing.

"Then that is something that you need to change," Dimitri said.

They were standing in the starting hold position with their bodies lightly touching. As it was, according to Dimitri, they were not nearly close enough. They had already spent twenty minutes following Dimitri and learning to do the basic steps on their own. Now they just had to put them together.

"Now, slow, slow, quick, quick, slow," Dimitri said.

They moved together, doing the right steps, but it was stiff and awkward. They kept it up for a minute as they maneuvered carefully around the room.

"Okay, stop," Dimitri said, sounding frustrated. "You're doing the steps but you're missing the entire point of the dance. It's like you're afraid to touch each other and you can't be afraid. Look, Dr. Carpenter warned me that this might be an issue for you two, so let's try to make this a game, shall we?"

"How?" Cindy asked.

Dimitri walked over. "I will make you a little bet, yes? I bet you that I can turn you on faster than you can turn Jeremiah on."

"What?" Cindy bleated, sounding fully panicked.

"Look, you are the woman, the seductress. It should be easy for you to turn any man on. You should be able to do it with a simple swish of your hip, with the sweep of your leg, with the passion in your eyes. It should be much harder for the man to do the same to you, yes? But I bet I can get your interest, faster than you can get his."

Jeremiah wasn't sure if he was amused or offended by the entire situation. He could dance and dance well. He'd grown up in Israel and there was always dancing at celebrations. He'd taken more formal dance training as an adult. It helped with strength, agility, balance. And it never hurt to be able to know how to do it if you needed to attend an embassy gala, though most of his work had kept him much more in the shadows than that.

"What are we betting?" Cindy asked.

"A bottle of champagne to the winner?"

"Make it a bottle of sparkling cider and a box of chocolates and you're on," Cindy said, gritting her teeth.

Dimitri turned to Jeremiah with an apologetic expression. "My friend, I apologize, but I am doing this for your benefit."

Jeremiah nodded. "I understand. It should at least prove...interesting."

Cindy's throat was dry as Dimitri started the music and then approached her. He took her in his arms and held her body close to his, much closer than she and Jeremiah had been. "Our bodies should mold to each other, move together," he said. "Slow, slow, quick, quick, slow."

Then they were moving across the floor. At first it was a bit jerky, but the tighter he held her, and the more she forced herself to relax, the smoother their gait became until it felt like they were moving as one person.

"Trust me. I am the man, I will lead. You will know through my movements where you are to go, what you are to do," Dimitri said softly, his voice almost hypnotic. "Close your eyes."

"But-"

"Ssh, just feel the music. You need to let go."

Cindy closed her eyes and within moments her other senses seemed to spring to vivid life. And for just a moment she let herself forget that she was dancing with Dimitri. And in the next moment they glided to a gentle stop.

"What is it?" she asked, opening her eyes.

"One minute, fifteen seconds," Dimitri said with a grin. "Let us see you beat that."

"But, how will you know how Jeremiah is feeling?" she asked.

"You will know, and in the way he moves I will know as well," Dimitri assured her.

Her heart was hammering as she walked over to Jeremiah. He took her in his arms and she pressed her body against his. She tried to think of the things that Dimitri had said about the swish of a hip and the sweep of a leg.

You can do this, Cindy. You can be sexy.

Dimitri started the music and she pressed her body harder against Jeremiah's as they began to move across the floor. She focused on maintaining contact as much as she could. She stared deep into Jeremiah's eyes and she could feel a fire starting to burn in her stomach. Her heart was racing, her breathing was becoming more shallow.

Jeremiah dipped her. It wasn't a move Dimitri had taught them, but she went with it, arching her back slightly. The music stopped and Jeremiah slowly brought her back to a standing position.

Dimitri clapped. "Twenty-five seconds. Very good. I owe you sparkling cider and chocolates. It was well done."

Cindy blushed as she pulled away from Jeremiah. She dropped her eyes, suddenly feeling too shy to look at him.

By the end of the session Dimitri seemed pleased with their progress. They moved on to their next small group session and it went better than the last one had. When they were done with that they walked out toward the pool and sat on a couple of the lawn chairs.

"I think we need to get a look at Dr. Carpenter's files," Cindy said. It was something she had been thinking increasingly about.

"I've been thinking about that, too. There's a chance the killers forgot to get rid of those or didn't want to risk arousing Dr. Carpenter's suspicions," Jeremiah said.

"Either way we should be able to check it out later tonight."

"Someone's coming," Jeremiah said, turning his head suddenly.

Cindy didn't hear anything, but sure enough, a few seconds later Jack appeared on the trail. He waved when he saw them.

"How's it going, Jack?" Jeremiah asked.

"Good, I'm just looking for my wife. You seen her by any chance?"

"No," Cindy said. "How long has she been gone?"

"We got out of our therapy session with that crackpot doc over half an hour ago. She took a walk to let off some steam. I figured she'd end up back at the room, but I haven't seen her."

"He put you through the wringer?" Cindy guessed.

"Oh, man, that guy is nuts. Certifiably loony if you want my opinion. By the end I just wanted to put my fist through a wall, you know?"

"Sorry to hear that," Jeremiah said.

"Yeah, I think our next session with him I'll conveniently be experiencing a headache or something like that. I figure no sane person puts themselves through his special brand of torture twice."

"Dinner's in about ten minutes, I'm sure Jill will show up there if nothing else," Cindy said.

"Great, more of her and Kim gossiping, that's just what a guy needs."

"Well, if we see her, we'll tell her you're looking for her."

"Yeah, thanks. Catch you guys around."

Jack turned and ambled away.

Cindy and Jeremiah shared a silent look. They were clearly both glad not to be that couple.

"I guess we can start walking," Cindy said as she got up.

Jeremiah grabbed her hand and they headed toward the main building. They had only gone a few feet when a sudden scream split the air.

18

"What is that?" Cindy gasped.

"I think it came from one of the suites," Jeremiah said.

They started running in that direction. The scream stopped abruptly and that was almost worse.

They reached one of the suites just in time to see Dorothea emerge, eyes wide in terror.

"What is it?" Jeremiah demanded.

"A snake in my jewelry box!" the woman cried, pointing back inside.

Cindy paused, "A snake?"

"Yes!"

Jeremiah ran inside and Cindy forced herself to follow. Flynn was backing out of the doorway that led from the living room to the bedroom, his face ashen.

"There is a snake," he said, pointing.

As soon as he got out of the doorway Jeremiah walked into the bedroom. As much as she didn't want to deal with a snake, Cindy forced herself to walk in after him and Flynn followed.

On the dresser was a small travel sized jewelry box, and, just as Dorothea had said, there was a small snake slithering through the jewelry.

"How on earth did it get there?" Cindy asked.

"I think someone put it there," Jeremiah said grimly.

"Why would anyone do that?" Flynn asked.

Cindy could hear raised voices outside. Clearly others had heard the scream and had come running as well.

"I don't know, but the snake isn't poisonous," Jeremiah said.

He picked the snake up and Cindy and Flynn stepped back, giving him plenty of room. Then they followed him back through the living room and outside. Several people had gathered and most of them shrank back as Jeremiah walked through them with the snake. Moments later he was letting it go into some bushes.

"Ewww, why didn't you kill it?" Kim asked.

Jeremiah stared at her. "It would have been disrespectful."

"What are you talking about?" she asked.

"This is reservation land that we are on. To the Native Americans, all life is precious. The snake wasn't poisonous and it posed no threat. I just returned it to its environment. I would very much like to know how it ended up in there," he said, looking back at the suite.

"Slithered, no doubt," Jill said with an exaggerated shudder.

"By the way, Jill, your husband is looking for you," Cindy said.

"What?" Jill asked, looking startled at suddenly having attention on her.

Cindy turned away and watched as Dorothea went back into the suite. She emerged just a few seconds later. "My pearl necklace is gone!"

"Are you sure?" Arnold asked as he pushed his way forward from the back of the crowd.

"Yes. I opened my jewelry box because I was going to wear the necklace to dinner. That's when I saw the snake inside."

"Was the necklace still there at that point?" Arnold asked.

Cindy bristled at the question. It could be seen as an implication that she or Jeremiah had taken the necklace when they'd been in the room after the discovery of the snake.

"I have no idea," Dorothea said.

Arnold glanced at Jeremiah and Cindy, before he could say anything, though, Flynn spoke up.

"It couldn't have been. I was in there with Cindy and Jeremiah when Jeremiah removed the snake. No one else has been in that room."

"So, maybe whoever took the necklace left the snake as a distraction," Cindy said.

"That would only work if the thief needed time to get away, leave the resort," Jeremiah said.

"So, we just need to find out if anyone's missing," Tristan said from his place further back in the crowd.

"No one has left and no one is leaving," Arnold said, irritation heavy in his voice. "And let's stop throwing around words. We don't know that someone took the necklace. It's probably simply been misplaced or lost somehow. Dorothea, when did you last see it?"

"Last night when I took it off and put it away before getting ready for bed," she said.

"Are you sure you put it away? Maybe you put it somewhere else without thinking or lost it before you got back to the suite?"

She folded her arms across her chest and her eyes glared daggers at him. "Young man, I am quite certain," she said, nearly spitting the words at him.

Cindy had already liked Dorothea, but now she really liked her.

"Alright, why don't the two of you come with me to the office, and we'll try and get to the bottom of this," Arnold said. "Everyone else, head in to dinner."

Dorothea and Flynn closed their door and followed Arnold.

Reluctantly Cindy and Jeremiah followed the rest to the dining room.

"My money is on Jill, she's been eyeing that necklace since the first night and her husband couldn't find her a while ago," Cindy whispered to Jeremiah.

"You might be right. Kim was there with her. It could have even been the two of them."

"Who do you think took her necklace?" Beth asked as soon as she and Tristan were seated at the dinner table with Cindy and Jeremiah.

"I don't know," Cindy said, not wanting to show her hand.

"Jill and Kim have both been awfully obsessed with it," Tristan said.

"You think either of them is capable of picking up a snake?" Beth asked skeptically.

"Good point. Unless the whole squeamish thing is an act."

"Everything about those two seems fake to me," Beth said.

"Well, hopefully it will all be sorted out by the time we finish dinner," Jeremiah said.

"Just in time for another group session," Tristan said with a sigh. "Oh, well, it could be worse."

"We could have another session with Dr. Carpenter," Beth said.

"We had the two o'clock session with Dr. Carpenter. Man, did he put us through the ringer," Tristan said while Beth nodded. "He ultimately told us that we needed to get separate hobbies so that there was an area of our lives that didn't have overlap which would be good for us as individuals and a couple apparently."

"We had the four o'clock session with him yesterday," Cindy said.

"What did he tell you guys?" Beth asked.

"That we needed to engage in more public displays of affection."

Tristan laughed. "Wow, you got an easy one. Trade you?"

"Not even!" Cindy said.

And despite what he had told them to do there had still been very little public or private displays of affection. Granted, there was a lot going on, but still.

An obnoxious idea hit her. She slipped off her shoe under the table. Then she stretched out her foot and rubbed it against the inside of Jeremiah's calf. He jumped and turned to look at her, clearly startled.

She smirked. "Doctor's orders," she said.

Mark jerked awake as he heard his cell phone ringing. He was disoriented and for a moment had no idea where he was. Then it came back to him as he recognized the wood of his desk at work, wood that now had a little puddle of drool on it.

He sat up and something fell off his back and onto the floor. He picked it up. It was a piece of paper with the words "Do not wake until children are in college".

"Very funny," he called out, waving the paper in the air.

Around the room other officers burst out laughing.

He was awake. But why? It seemed to him there had been a reason why.

His phone trilled. A message. Joseph had called and left a message.

He pulled the phone up to his ear and dialed Joseph back. The other man answered on the first ring.

"Joseph, what do you have for me?" Mark asked.

"Eric Wilson called me back. He told me that what Marcia said was true, except for the fact that her lawyer was better than his. What was significant, though, was that he told me a couple of members of the staff enticed him to enter a high stakes poker game at the casino. They drove him there, went with him, and he did lose big. He also figured that there had been cheating going on although he couldn't figure out how."

"Did he say anything?"

"No, he figured it out at the end when he got wiped out while holding four queens. He said by the time he wised up he realized what kind of people he was dealing with and he figured if he made a fuss he might end up dead."

"If only Malcolm had the same insight he might still be alive."

"Yeah. It sounds like these are bad dudes. I hope that helps."

"It does. Do you think Eric would be willing to testify about any of that in court?"

"He might be persuaded. For either money or ego. If he had a chance of getting some of his money back or having it shown that he was cheated it would help. He fancies himself quite the sophisticated card player and anything that would help restore that reputation would be appealing to him."

"I'll keep that in mind."

Mark hung up and staggered to his feet. He needed to go home. He glared as several officers continued to snicker. He would get back at all of them.

After he got some sleep.

Which at the rate things were going might be when the twins went off to college.

"I hate you guys," he said to the nearest cluster of men who just laughed.

Dinner was halfway through and still Dorothea and Flynn had not appeared. Jeremiah was on edge. With everything else they had going on the last thing they needed was one of the other guests playing jewel thief. It could be a simple case of monkey see, monkey want, but it didn't feel quite right to him. The addition of the snake was too deliberate, almost like a message of some sort.

Movement just outside the door of the room caught his eye. It was the masseuse, the one Dorothea and Flynn had said was a fairly new addition to the staff. He looked like he was trying to get someone's attention. He was not as discreet as he probably thought he was.

A few moments later across the room both Jack and Levi got up and strolled toward the lobby. They were trying to look casual and Levi was failing miserably at it.

Jeremiah stood up and pulled his phone out of his pocket. He held it up to his ear. "Yeah, what is it?" he asked as he ended up walking out of the room slightly ahead of the other two men.

"No, it's going fine. Wait, say that again, I couldn't quite hear you," Jeremiah said, pausing and holding his free hand up to his other ear.

Jack and Levi joined the masseuse and all three moved into the gym. Jeremiah moved quietly up against the wall just outside the door, and leaned against it, still holding the phone to his ear like he was listening to someone.

"We're still set, right?" Levi was saying.

"We're good to go if you are," the masseuse said. "We have it all set up so that after dinner tomorrow night both ladies will be having serious girl time, massages, facials, the works. They won't miss you for hours."

"This is great. I've been dying for some action," Jack said.

"We've got the hottest poker game this side of the country. You gentlemen are just lucky you earned yourselves a couple of seats," the masseuse said. "As soon as dinner is over tomorrow, you'll meet our guy out front and then you'll be in poker heaven."

Jeremiah quickly moved away. He'd heard enough and lingering longer just added to the risk of being caught. He put his phone back in his pocket as he returned to the table. No sooner had he done so than he felt it vibrate. He pulled it back out and saw that Mark was calling.

He answered. "Hey, it's not a great time."

"Fine. I only have three words for you: rigged poker game."

"I'm right there with you," Jeremiah said. "I'll call later."

Cindy was staring at him wide-eyed and he could tell that curiosity was killing her. He reached over, grabbed her hand, and gave it a squeeze. Out of the corner of his eye he saw Jack and Levi returning to the dining room.

"How about we skip dessert and get a walk in before the next meeting?" he suggested.

Cindy nodded vigorously and a minute later they were outside heading for their bungalow. Once in there he filled her in on what he'd learned.

"Do you think Malcolm knew they cheated and threatened to expose them so they killed him?" she asked.

"That's sounding more and more possible. I mean, if they're taking people for millions, they're not going to want anyone messing that up for them."

"So, there are conspirators here and at the casino," Cindy mused.

"Yes. We need to get over there and figure out exactly what's going on."

Mark called again and Jeremiah put his phone on speaker as he gave them the rest of the story. Then he asked for Kyle's number which Cindy was able to give him before hanging up again.

"He does not sound alright," Jeremiah commented.

"I don't think he's slept in a while."

"Okay, back to that casino. Maybe we can sneak over there tonight," Jeremiah said.

"First we have to go to the last session of the night, back with the whole group."

Jeremiah rolled his eyes. "Can't you just fake a headache or something and get us out of it?"

"I doubt it. Besides we don't want to draw even more attention to ourselves than need be."

"You're right," he said with a sigh. "Now's not the time to rush and ruin everything."

"What we need to do is figure out a way to get you into that poker game," Cindy said.

"Sorry, not me, I can't play."

"You must play poker," she said.

"No. Baccarat, yes. Poker, no."

"Spies really play baccarat?" she asked.

"It's kind of a prerequisite when working in some countries. Or a badge of honor. Either way, yes, I play baccarat."

"You'll have to show me sometime."

"We'll have to get Joseph to bankroll us. It's an expensive game. But for now what we need to focus on is getting *you* in that poker game," Jeremiah said.

"I have no money."

"We'll call Joseph and Mark, I'm sure they can arrange something."

"Yeah, but I've never played for actual money."

"But at least you've played, and we don't have time or opportunity for you to teach me everything you know about poker. You're our best shot," Jeremiah said.

"Okay, but even so, I don't see it happening. I can't exactly walk up to someone and say 'Hey, deal me in.' You know?"

"No, but I've got a way that they'll come to you."

"How?" she asked.

Jeremiah smiled. "By doing what couples have done for thousands of years. We're going to fight about money."

19

The group session that night ended up being canceled as staff were apparently called together to help find Dorothea's necklace. As much as Cindy wanted to help with that, she had more pressing issues to deal with. Jeremiah went out for a little while to follow spy on Summer and the woman from the front desk, but was back shortly. He was convinced that because of all the other activity going on that no one would have a chance to sneak off and dig up a body.

Cindy spent time steeling herself mentally for the challenges the next day were going to bring. At least by the time the first morning session rolled around she was ready.

Cindy was certain that Jeremiah was out of his mind. That was the only possible explanation. She'd listened carefully to his plan, though, and ultimately she couldn't find fault with it. They approached the building where they were about to have a group session. It was show time.

"You ready?" Jeremiah asked softly.

"I am."

Louder Jeremiah said, "I just think it's the man's responsibility to take care of his wife."

"You're living a couple of generations in the past then," Cindy said, also elevating her voice.

"We should be able to live on what I can bring in," Jeremiah said as he reached forward and grabbed the handle of the door. He yanked it open.

"And that's stupid. There's no reason for us to live like paupers," Cindy said.

"Modest, yes, but we won't be living like paupers. Just because it doesn't meet up with your high standards-"

She cut Jeremiah off. "Wait, are you saying that I'm a snob? Because you know, I've never treated you any differently because you didn't have money."

They had the attention of everyone in the room.

"Don't say it like that, you make me sound like a bum who is homeless on the street."

"I'm not calling you a bum, I'm just saying that your Spartan lifestyle might work for you, but not for me. And it doesn't have to, which is the great thing."

"We shouldn't be using your money to pay our monthly expenses. That should come from my salary."

"Which would mean having to move into your tiny apartment, and that's never going to happen. I realize this is probably some weird macho crap that they taught you in Israel growing up, but here in America-"

"Here in America a man can still have his dignity and pride," Jeremiah snapped. "I've seen the way your family spends money and that's not for me. I want no part of their money."

"We're not talking about their money, we're talking about my money."

"Oh, yes, how could I ever forget that you're rich and I'm not?" Jeremiah was shouting now.

"What is wrong with you?" Cindy yelled, balling her hands into fists at her side.

"Cindy! Jeremiah! Deep breaths. Let's just try to calm down," Arnold said, hurrying over to them. "I know income inequity can cause stress, but-"

"This has nothing to do with income inequity. She's never worked a day in her life. She inherited her grandparents' fortune."

"I'm tired of doing things his way. You know we're stuck in a teeny little bungalow because he insisted on paying for half of this retreat? If I'd let him pay for the whole thing like he wanted to then he'd still be saving for months, maybe years before we got here. Lucky me, we were only dating, so he couldn't make the 'responsible for paying for his family' argument stick."

"Maybe it's lucky for both of us that we're here. It makes some things a lot clearer," Jeremiah said, sounding incredibly angry.

"I don't like you like this," Cindy said, crossing her arms.

"Then maybe we shouldn't be dating."

"Maybe we shouldn't. We came here to see where we should go from here as a couple and I think things are becoming pretty clear."

"Okay, that's enough. You need to either settle down or one of you needs to walk away so that the two of you can calm down and get a chance to think before you say anything else hurtful," Arnold said.

"Good idea. I think I'll go see what else there is to do around this dump," Cindy fumed before turning and storming out the door. "If anyone wants me I'll be at the pool," she threw back over her shoulder before letting the door slam behind her.

She kept walking, keeping her head high, and headed straight for the bungalow. There she'd change into her bathing suit and head for the pool area in case anyone did want to come looking. She was just grateful that Jeremiah was the one stuck in the room with everyone who had just witnessed their fake fight.

Jeremiah watched Cindy walk out of the room. It surprised him how much even fake fighting with her caused him anxiety. He had an almost overwhelming need to chase after her even though he knew she really wasn't angry and that this was all part of the plan.

He took a deep breath, grimaced, and turned to Arnold. "Coming from two different worlds can be exciting at first."

Arnold nodded. "But sooner or later if you're going to stay together you have to pick one to live in."

"That's very well put," he said in a moment of sincerity.

"Thank you." Arnold turned. "Class, we'll begin in five minutes." He turned back to Jeremiah. "Excuse me for a moment."

Jeremiah watched as Arnold left the building, hopefully on the way to tell someone that Cindy was rich.

He turned back and saw that all the other couples were still staring.

"Dude, you should totally let her pay for stuff," Tristan said.

"And there's no way she should have to move into a dinky apartment," Jill said, wrinkling her nose.

Jeremiah sighed. Unfortunately being the one who stayed behind meant a lot of awkwardness, but better that he endure it than Cindy.

"It's hard, sometimes. We are so different. Different cultures, different values," he said, purposely allowing his natural accent to manifest more strongly. "We don't always understand each other."

"You don't always have to understand each other," Beth said earnestly. "You just have to love each other."

"That's right," Tristan said, picking up his wife's hand and kissing it.

"And what Arnold said about picking a world? Trust me, Cindy's world sounds a whole lot better," Jack said.

Jill nodded emphatically.

Jeremiah didn't say anything else. He slowly sat down on his cushion on the floor and stared at Cindy's empty one. He had no idea what he was supposed to do here by himself, but he figured that was Arnold's job to figure out. The instructor should be back shortly and would surely tell him what to do. Personally he was hoping to be excused which meant he could do a little more reconnaissance work, and maybe even be able to keep an eye on Cindy while she was at the pool.

Cindy's heart was still beating a little faster than normal by the time she'd changed into her bathing suit. As she glanced in the mirror she was grateful that Dave had talked her into buying a new one. Her old suit would never have passed muster as belonging to a woman with money. Or probably even one with taste. She shook her head ruefully. She could thank Dave for her entire wardrobe this week, which was giving her the chance to play out this charade.

She grabbed a hat, towel, and some sunscreen and headed for the pool. Fortunately it had been a warm week even if it was February. That was one of the nice things about living in southern California, it rarely got truly cold.

As she walked to the pool she tried to put a little angry woman with attitude swagger into her walk in case anyone was looking. She made it all the way there without encountering anyone. It was fairly isolated on the property, though, and theoretically everyone should be in sessions for a couple of hours. She ignored the beach chairs that were scattered around and instead spread out her towel on the sand and stretched out. She'd wait a few minutes before applying sunscreen. Hopefully someone would approach her in that time and she'd be back inside before she needed it.

It hadn't been as difficult faking an argument with Jeremiah as she'd thought it would be. The really hard part had been keeping it on topic. She'd found that as she raised her voice and faked the anger that there was a lot of real frustration bubbling just beneath the surface. She wished they could be more like a normal couple and it was getting harder and harder to keep their relationship a secret. She was trying to respect his need to do so, but it was starting to get to her.

If anything this retreat was bringing the frustration and impatience to the surface. Maybe it was being around so many married couples who were honestly trying to work on their relationships instead of being here clandestinely trying to investigate a disappearance. Or maybe it was the fact that here they were getting to hold hands and kiss openly. They were even expected to and in some cases required to. It made the secrecy back home seem that much more oppressive and it made her less and less eager to return to her real life. She couldn't get what Dr. Carpenter had said about sacrificing everything else for safety out of her mind.

"Hey, how are you doing?"

Cindy looked up to see Summer, the yoga instructor, looking down at her sympathetically.

"I'm okay," Cindy said, being careful not to smile as she propped herself up on her elbows.

Summer sat down on the sand next to her. "Come on, Sweetie, you don't have to put on a brave face. You're safe. There's nothing you can say to me that will ever be repeated."

"Jeremiah and I had a fight," Cindy said.

"I heard," Summer said, tilting her head to the side. "Want to talk about it?"

"Wow, gossip travels fast around here."

"It's not like that. Arnold was worried about you, but he had to teach the class. He asked me to come make sure you were okay. Plus, he thought you might be more willing to talk to another woman."

"Wow, a man actually came up with a good idea all on his own," Cindy said sarcastically. "I wouldn't have made a bet on that."

Summer laughed and put her hand on Cindy's arm. "Yeah, most of the time they can be pretty stupid."

She was trying to make Cindy feel comfortable, reel her in and get her to confide. It was possible she was just a kind person and a good counselor, but Cindy was hoping that Summer's attention had a more sinister motivation.

"And my guy trumps them all," Cindy said with a sigh.

"What did he do?"

"He comes across all King of Hearts until he has to actually face that I'm the Queen of Diamonds." Cindy was purposefully using as many card and gambling related words and phrases as she could, just to make sure the other woman was connecting her with gambling.

"So, he's all lovey dovey until he realizes that what you need is to see a ring then he gets cold feet?" Summer asked, clearly trying to catch up.

"I'm sorry. I'm used to playing things close to the vest. I don't often like to come right out and lay my cards on the table for everyone to see. I'm not looking for a ring from him. Well, I mean, eventually, I think. That's kind of why we're here to explore whether or not we're suited for each other. I come from money. He hates it when people know that, so I try to keep it concealed when we're places people don't already know us."

"That seems very strange. Why would he hate that you come from money?"

"He's got these weird ideas that the man should take care of everything, earn the money, all that. I mean, I thought it was cute at first, but then he started getting really weird about it. I don't know what his problem is. It's money, it's meant to be spent and enjoyed."

"And you're not getting to spend your own money?" Summer asked, eyes wide.

"Exactly! Take this retreat for example. I wanted us to go to this nice place up in Napa, you know, a real first class place. I was happy to pay for it, but because he couldn't at least pay his own way he refused. That's how we ended up in this dump. It was all he could afford." Cindy winced. "I'm sorry. I did not mean to slam this place. You and the other staff have been very nice."

"No, it's okay. I understand. We make do with what we have here and we're not like one of the really fancy retreat centers."

"I know. And in theory the laid back thing sounds nice, but there's just nothing interesting to do and I'm so bored."

"I'm sorry to hear that," Summer said.

Cindy was hoping Summer would say something useful soon. She was beginning to worry that she was in danger of overplaying her hand. She sighed in a dramatic fashion. "You know what I really want right now?"

"Tell me."

"I want to blow off the retreat, Jeremiah, all of it and just go do something fun."

"Then I think you should," Summer said emphatically.

Cindy laughed. "Great. Got any suggestions?"

Summer looked at her, eyes narrowing slightly. "You know I might be able to come up with something fun. Let me see what I can do."

"Oh, please, yes. That would be fantastic."

Summer stood abruptly. "I've got to go take care of a few things. Tell you what, though. I'll check in with you after dinner."

"Okay. I'll probably be here until then."

"Great. Take it easy, and try to relax a little. No one's going to bother you here. You should have the place to yourself for a couple of hours at the very least."

"Thanks," Cindy said.

Summer left and as Cindy laid back down she hoped that by the end of the day someone would be approaching her with a poker invitation. She figured that she should at least give it a few minutes before she packed up and headed back to the bungalow, just in case Summer hadn't gone that far away.

After about five minutes had passed she opened her eyes as she debated about going inside. She was surprised to see Jeremiah heading toward her wearing swim trunks and a short-sleeved button down shirt and carrying a towel of his own.

He laid his towel down next to hers and then sat down on it. "TK told me the session wouldn't be useful to me without my partner present. I told him I was going to try and talk to you."

"So, people won't be surprised to see you here."

"If anyone does."

"Summer came to see me. Arnold told her about the fight."

"Did she say anything?"

"Not directly, but when she left she promised to try and find me something fun to do and that we'd talk after dinner. I all but asked her if she knew of any big poker games so if she doesn't come back with something she's either out of the loop completely or I managed to scare her off."

"I'm sure you were fine. I guess now we just have to wait and see. At least we can be comfortable for a while and we got out of that session."

He laid down, stretching out.

She turned on her side to stare at him. "You know I must say that despite all the circumstances, this is very romantic."

"I guess," he said.

She reached out and touched his cheek and he turned to look at her.

"You haven't commented on my bikini," she said.

"It looks very nice."

Nice? Nice was not what she'd been going for. She'd never owned a bikini in her life and it had taken all her courage to get and wear this one. It was black, it was tiny, and it had a dusting of little rhinestones. Nice was not a good answer, not with all the emotions that had been swirling around inside her.

She leaned over and kissed him. After a couple of seconds he moved. "We shouldn't be kissing in public," he said.

"Um, we're supposed to be kissing here, even Dr. Carpenter thinks so. It's even part of our cover. It's weird if we don't. And besides, this can barely be described as being public."

"Yes, but we shouldn't get used to it. If we get used to kissing in public here then we might slip up back home."

"And that would be bad?" she questioned.

"Yes."

She stood up abruptly. For a moment she thought of leaving, heading back to the bungalow, but he would just follow her. If she couldn't be alone at the moment then they had some things they needed to work out.

"Are you embarrassed to let others know that we have feelings for each other?" she asked.

"Of course not."

"Well, you're acting like you are."

He stood up and moved closer to her, lowering his voice a bit. "Once it's out there for the world to know things are going to change."

"Yes. We won't have to keep lying to everyone, and we could actually have a real relationship."

"It's more than that. As my...girlfriend...you're going to come under a lot of intense scrutiny from my congregation and yours. It could get uncomfortable."

"So?"

He took a deep breath. "Cindy, it's not too late to change your mind about me, about us."

And somehow that was the worst thing he could have said to her at the moment. The anger that she'd been struggling to hold back crashed down around her.

"Do you regret what you said to me back in Jerusalem?"

"No," he said.

"Have *you* changed *your* mind about your feelings for me?"

"No."

"Prove it," she said, her breath catching in her throat.

He tilted his head to the side. "How?"

She leaned into him, tilted her head up and kissed him. His lips barely moved against hers. The fact that he wasn't even kissing her back made her even angrier and more than a little frightened.

"Do you remember what you told me?" she asked as she pulled away.

He nodded gravely. "I told you that I belonged to you: heart, mind, and body. That everything I am is yours."

"If you really believe that, then I have the right to do this." She raised her hands to his chest and unbuttoned the top button of his shirt. She slid her hands down to the second and undid it as well. She was playing a dangerous game with him, but she needed to know that he was serious, that he still meant everything he'd said to her.

He didn't move, just stared at her with veiled eyes. When the last button was undone she pulled his shirt open and ran her hands up and down his chest, thrilling to the feel of his muscles under her fingertips. After a few seconds he said softly, "Cindy, don't."

"Don't?" she asked, glaring at him. She dropped her hands. "Okay, I get it now. Do you want out, you just don't want to say so, and what, hurt my feelings? You know what's hurting me? It's this. You saying you care, but then acting like you don't. I don't know what the problem is. Maybe it's that I'm not Jewish, and I get that, I really do, but say so. Maybe you don't find me attractive now that our lives aren't in danger. Maybe you kissed me and got it out of your system and now you just don't know how to tell me it's over."

She was shaking now as she glared at him. "I've been patient with you, *Malachi*," she said, purposely using that name. "But I love you. I've loved you for a very long time, and I'm tired of keeping that a secret. If you don't love me or you're ashamed of me or are too worried about what other people are going to say, then I can make your life easier."

"How do you think you could possibly make my life easier?" he asked, sounding strangled.

She stared him in the eyes. "I release you from whatever obligation you feel toward me. I love you too much to live a lie with you, so I'll walk away now and save you the trouble of leaving me later."

Cindy turned to go.

"Cindy!"

She paused. "What?" she asked without turning around.

"I don't want you to walk away."

"Then don't let me."

"What can I say?"

She shook her head. "At this point, nothing. Talk is cheap, especially for someone who lies as well as you do."

She realized it was harsh, but now was not the time to hold back what she was feeling.

Jeremiah couldn't take his eyes off Cindy. She looked stunning in the bikini and he was still reeling from the feel of her hands on his chest. It had taken every ounce of control he had not to do something rash in that moment. Now he was stunned by what she was saying. And through his confusion one thing became clear. She truly didn't understand how he felt about her, and it was his fault.

"Cindy, let me explain," he said, his mouth feeling dry and his heart beginning to race in fear.

She turned away. She was leaving. Not because she didn't love him, but because he had held back too much. He couldn't let her go, not like this. He stepped forward, grabbed her arm and spun her around. He wrapped both arms around her, bent her backwards so that he was supporting her weight, and kissed her hard.

She came alive in his arms. She was kissing with the kind of abandon he dreamed about at night. He straightened her up, put her back on her own feet, but she clung to him, kissing him deeper, faster, her lips warm and moist against his.

And every last shred of self-control he had vanished. He shrugged off his shirt. He sank down onto the beach blanket and pulled her down on top of him. He could feel the bare skin of her stomach against his, their legs tangled. He kissed her until they were both gasping for breath.

Her eyes were closed and he let his hands roam down her back and onto her hips. "Look at me," he said, his voice husky.

She opened her eyes and stared at him.

"I never lied about what I feel for you," he said.

"Given the last several months, how could I know that? You push me away and then you pull me close only to push me away again."

"I love you, Cindy. And you should know this. Not a day goes by that I don't fantasize about well, you know what about. I'm only human, after all."

"I fantasize about that, too," she said.

Just hearing her admit that almost destroyed the last fragile thread of rational thought left to him. He closed his eyes, struggling to keep it together.

"I understand that I've put artificial boundaries on us as a couple. I'm sorry for that. But I never want you to think it's because I don't love you or don't want you. And I promise to do a better job of letting you know how I feel if you'll do one thing for me."

"What's that?" she asked.

"Get up right now and walk away before something happens that we'll both regret."

He opened his eyes and looked up at her. For one heart-stopping moment he thought she was going to refuse. Slowly, though, she nodded, and then she pushed herself up and a moment later was on her feet.

He stared up at her.

"It is a fantastic bathing suit," he said.

A smile lit up her face. "You really like it?"

"Yes, do me a favor?"

"What?" she asked.

"Don't let me see it again for a while."

She picked up her towel and wrapped it around herself with deliberate, exaggerated motions. "I think I can do that."

"I'd appreciate it. Could you hand me my shirt?"

She picked it up and shook the sand off of it. "No, I'm sorry. I'm keeping it."

"You're what?" he asked.

"You heard me. I'm the girlfriend. By California law that gives me the right to steal shirts, sweatshirts and possibly a really cool leather jacket."

"Oh you think so?"

"I know so," she said with a smirk.

"That seems to be a bit one sided to me."

She shrugged. "Tough. Deal with it."

"And California law allows me to steal what of yours?"

"Nothing."

"That seems very inequitable," he said as he stood to his feet. "I think perhaps I should impose a tickle tax."

She shrieked and danced out of reach as he lunged toward her.

"But you have been warned," he said. "You don't know when, you don't know where, but you will be tickled mightily."

She giggled and he couldn't help but smile like an idiot.

He scooped up his towel, threw it over his shoulders in an attempt to at least cover some of his scars, and then grabbed her hand. Together they walked back toward their bungalow. The small group sessions were still going so they didn't see anyone on their walk. At last they made it back to their bungalow.

Cindy had pulled his keycard out of the pocket of his shirt, which she was still fiercely holding on to. She inserted it into the slot and a second later was pushing open the door.

The moment they stepped inside Jeremiah held up a hand and Cindy looked at him questioningly. He pressed a finger to his lips to signal for her to be quiet.

Someone had broken into their room.

20

Mark woke up on the couch in the living room with no memory of how he'd gotten there. He was still in his clothes, including his jacket. Buster was laying on his feet which might explain why they seemed to have gone completely numb. His cell phone, a pad of paper with some numbers scribbled on it, and a pen were on the floor next to the couch.

"Traci?" he called out, his throat dry and hoarse feeling.

Traci walked into the room. "Look who's up," she said.

"What happened?" he asked.

"Only the most epic case of sleep policing I've ever seen," she said with a smile.

"What?"

"You were actually working in your sleep. I thought you were awake, but not so much as it turned out. When you fell over on the couch I decided not to wake you."

"Thanks."

He stretched out his hand and managed to grab the pad of paper with two fingers and pull it closer. "This looks like a phone number, do you have any idea whose it is?"

"You called Kyle for Hank's number. That's it, assuming you actually wrote it down correctly, but given that you weren't actually conscious I'm not assuming much."

"Didn't that freak you out?" he asked.

"It would have, but I saw you do it in college that one time. Took notes the entire class and you were dead asleep."

Mark still had no memory of calling Kyle or writing down Hank's number. He didn't even remember getting home. "So not okay," he muttered to himself.

His stomach growled, proof that he had missed at least one meal. "Come on, Buster, I have to sit up," he told the Beagle.

The dog jumped down and Mark tried to sit up. Fire raced through his feet as the nerves came stingingly back to life.

"Oh, by the way, you had this on your back when you came home. I'm guessing some of the guys at the station had something to do with it," she said, handing him a small piece of paper with tape stuck on it. He read it.

Your tax dollars at work.

"I'm going to get those guys," he said with a scowl as he crumpled it up.

"I'd take it as a good sign. No one's teased you since...everything."

She was right. He had effectively been persona non grata for a long time. The fact that they were teasing him was a sign that he was slowly being accepted back into the fold.

He picked up his phone and dialed the number on the paper. After a couple of rings a man answered.

"Hank?"

"Yeah."

"Hank, this is Detective Mark Walters. We met on a cattle drive-"

"I remember you, Mark. Why is it you're calling?"

"I seem to remember something about you growing up here in southern California."

"Yes."

"Do you by any chance have any connections to anyone on the reservation or the town of Pineneedle which is right outside it?"

"You think all us Indians know each other?" Hank asked.

Mark cursed himself for calling anyone when he still wasn't awake yet. "No, of course not. I know it's a long shot, but I'm desperately trying to find an in, someone who can help me solve a murder and keep Cindy and Jeremiah out of danger. I could have sworn at one point I heard you say something about Pineneedle."

"Detective, relax, I'm messing with you," Hank said.

"Good to know."

"I know you've got twins now, but you've got to get some more sleep, and don't lose your sense of humor."

"How do you know...never mind. Do you know anyone?"

"There's an officer on the police force there, Zeb Smith. He'll take on the tribal elders if you give him a good enough reason."

"Thanks, I appreciate it. Anything else I should know?"

"Yeah, Zeb cares about justice. He'll back you, but if you hold out on him he'll kick your butt halfway out of the state."

"Understood. Thanks."

He hung up and turned to look at Traci. "Did I do anything else when I got home last night that I should know about?"

"You called Joseph and told him to put money in a bank account for Cindy."

"Why would I do that?" Mark asked.

"You said something about a poker game."

"Crap," Mark said. He had been really out of it. He needed to call Jeremiah and find out what was happening. "Did I say how much money?"

Traci nodded. "Ten million."

Mark blinked. "Okay, now I'm awake."

Cindy stood quietly just inside the room while Jeremiah went through everything. She could tell that someone had been in their room from the signs he had given her. She had no idea how Jeremiah could tell, but somehow he knew.

At last he nodded, indicating that it was safe.

"What happened?" she asked.

"It's my guess that they were looking for this," he said, holding up the ATM card to the fake bank account that Mark had given her as part of her cover documents when they had first come to the resort.

Cindy had left the card and the fake driver's license in her purse here in the room.

"What makes you think that's what they were checking out?"

"When you first got them from Mark you put the driver's license in front. Now the ATM card is in the front."

Once again she was stunned by just how hyper-observant Jeremiah could be.

"Well, they didn't steal it. Do you think they just wanted the numbers off of it?"

"I would be willing to bet they called in to verify a large purchase transaction, just to be sure that you actually had the kind of money they're looking for. It's a good thing Mark had Joseph add funds to it."

"I don't like any of this," Cindy said.

"Neither do I, but if it means that you're about to get an invite to the game then it's a good thing."

Jeremiah's phone went off and he answered. "Hi, Mark. Yeah, we baited the trap. We'll see what we catch. I can already tell they're interested. The game is tonight so if they're going to make their move, it will have to be soon. Sure. We'll keep you in the loop."

"Now what?" Cindy asked as Jeremiah hung up.

"Now, we head to lunch."

"We still haven't managed to get a look at Dr. Carpenter's files," she pointed out.

"It was too risky last night with people tearing this place apart looking for Dorothea's necklace. If I get a chance today I'll try for it. Otherwise we'll just have to hope for the best after the fact."

"Okay, how are we playing lunch?" she asked.

"Cold."

Which meant no hand-holding she realized. It made sense, but it was frustrating. She was trying to enjoy physical contact with him while she could before they went home.

Again she silently lectured herself that she needed to focus on the bigger picture: capturing killers and getting justice for Malcolm and his wife. It was hard to focus, though. Everything just felt like it was coming to a head with Jeremiah.

"Okay, let's do lunch," she said, steeling herself for the experience.

They were nearly to the main building when Summer walked up to them. "Hey," she said, smiling at Cindy.

"Hi," Cindy said.

"Can I talk to you for just a sec?"

"Go ahead, I'll catch up," Cindy said to Jeremiah, trying to put a bit of ice in her voice.

"Whatever," he grumbled. He headed off and Cindy rolled her eyes.

"So, still not having any fun?" Summer said sympathetically.

"Zero," Cindy said with a sigh. "I think coming here was a mistake."

"Maybe not. Sometimes it's good to find things out about people before the relationship goes too far. You're at a perfect stage where it's still easy to walk away."

"I don't know, it's starting to look that way. You know I really thought he was the one?" Cindy said, sounding as despondent as she could. And just like that she felt herself tearing up. She took a shaky breath. All the relationship talk was hitting a little too close to home.

"Look, don't cry. I figured out something fun for you to do this evening and a way Mr. Cranky Pants won't even know what you're up to."

"Yeah?"

"Are you a gambler?"

Cindy laughed. "I took a chance on him, didn't I?"

Summer laughed, too, a high fake laugh that grated on Cindy's nerves.

"There's a very exclusive, high-level poker game for serious players over at the casino tonight. If you're interested, I can pull a few strings and get you in."

"Oh, that could be fun. Texas Hold 'Em, Draw or Stud?"

"Dealer's Choice."

"In a casino?"

"Like I said, it's a very exclusive game."

"Now you're talking my language," Cindy said.

"I thought I might be. Listen, after dinner meet out front of the main building."

"I'll be there."

"I have to run. I'll see you later."

Summer took off and Cindy continued on to the dining room. She nodded slightly to Jeremiah who was texting on his phone. She was in. Now the insanity could really begin.

After filling his captain in, Mark headed, with his blessings, for the town of Pineneedle, right on the edge of the reservation. Once there he drove straight to the small police station.

Inside he was pointed toward a desk in the back where a tall man with fair features and short black hair was poring over a report. He looked up as Mark approached.

"I'm Detective Mark Walters with the Pine Springs Police Department. Are you Zeb Smith?"

"I am. What can I do for you, Detective?"

Mark sat down across the desk from Zeb.

"A friend told me that you weren't afraid to go onto the reservation."

"I'm not afraid, but I don't go without good reason and solid evidence. It's not my business what goes on out there unless it has to be."

"I understand. Well, I have good reason and evidence, and there'll be more by end of day."

"I'll listen, but first tell me who this friend of yours is."

"His name is Hank Lightfoot, he grew up around here."

The officer broke out in a broad grin. "Why didn't you say you were a friend of Hank's in the beginning? It would have saved us a lot of fuss." He reached across the desk, offering his hand.

Mark shook it, relief flooding through him.

"Okay, so what's going on and what do you need from me?"

"We have reason to believe at least 4 employees of the resort out there are conspiring with a couple people from the casino to get some of the resort's rich clientele into a private high stakes poker game that's fixed. They're then splitting the profits amongst themselves."

The officer's expression grew angry as he listened. When Mark had finished he leaned forward. "That casino is owned by the entire tribe. The chief's nephew runs it and he's brought in a guy or two from the outside that I haven't felt any too comfortable with if you know what I mean. The resort is leasing the land they're on. They've been in business now for 15 years. The guy who owns it grew up with his grandfather on the reservation though you wouldn't know it to look at him. He went to a couple fancy colleges before setting up that business. He employees a lot of outsiders which doesn't always sit well with people. He's legit, though, I'd bet my life on it."

"How do you know?" Mark asked.

"I could give you a bunch of talk about knowing people, getting feelings about them like the good feeling that I got about you straight off. Truth is, though, I know Arnold pretty well. He's my brother. And let me tell you, if he caught his employees doing that he'd do more than just fire them. That's why I've got to be there, no matter what."

"I totally respect that," Mark said cautiously, "but we don't know yet that he's not involved."

"If it turns out he is, I'll arrest him myself. So, I assume you have a game plan in mind?"

"We do indeed. We've got someone in the poker game tonight."

"Ambitious," Zeb said, raising an eyebrow. "Is he any good?"

"She. And we're banking on it."

"What do you need from me?"

The afternoon passed in a blur. Jeremiah was told there had been a change in schedule and while Cindy was going to be having some spa like treatments that he had his choice of a couple of different activities. He opted for an extra session with Dr. Carpenter and then some time to just relax in the room.

They were getting ready for dinner and Cindy was a nervous wreck. Joseph had deposited an enormous amount of money into a bank account Mark had set up under her alias that she had been using at the retreat. She had never played for real money before and now she would be betting tens of thousands, maybe even hundreds of thousands on each hand. She would never have gambled with her own money, but the thought that she was gambling with someone else's just made it that much worse somehow. She kept telling herself that if everything went according to plan Joseph wouldn't be out a single cent.

"What should I wear?" she asked Jeremiah after she'd stood in front of the closet unable to make a decision for five minutes.

"Definitely the red one, it will keep the other gamblers distracted," he said.

"Really?"

He walked up behind her and wrapped his arms around her waist. "Really," he whispered into her ear before kissing it.

She turned in his arms and then he was kissing her lips. Her heart began to race as the kisses continued, deeper, more passionate. His breathing was ragged as he tightened his arms around her.

"Don't go," he whispered.

"What?"

"Don't go. Stay here with me," he said, his voice pleading.

"I have to go. This is our chance to catch the bad guys. It's why we're here," she said.

He put his hand under her chin and tilted her head upward so he could stare into her eyes. "Please, I'm begging you. Don't go. It's not safe. I...I can't protect you."

She stared back at him. "I know."

She stepped back, forcing him to release his hold on her.

After dinner Cindy was out in front of the building where both Jack and Levi seemed surprised to see her.

Inside she was in complete turmoil. She and Jeremiah hadn't spoken six words since she had told him she was going through with the plan. She owed it to Mark to do this. More than that, she owed it to herself.

A limo pulled up in front of them.

"Well, boys," Cindy said. "Let the games begin."

Mark, his captain, and Zeb were all on the casino floor, slowly running through their nickels as they kept watch. At last two men and a woman in a red dress were escorted through on their way to one of the private rooms.

It took all Mark's self-control not to stare. The woman was Cindy. She looked different than he'd ever seen her. She was cool, collected, and she was working her curves for all they were worth. It was like watching her doppelganger walk by; it was so hard to believe that it was the same woman he knew.

They hadn't been able to risk going near the resort to wire her up with a mic or anything. Fortunately Jeremiah had brought a whole bag of tricks with him unbeknownst to Mark and Cindy. The gold wristwatch Cindy was wearing was just a fancy casing for a panic button. As soon as she pushed it, Jeremiah would be alerted and he, in turn, would alert them. It wasn't ideal, but it was what it was.

Until she pushed that button all they could do was wait and wonder what was going on inside the room she had just disappeared into.

Cindy walked into the game room followed by Jack and Levi. Two other men were already present and seated at the table. A third man was standing in the corner and Cindy wasn't sure if he was running the room or providing security. Either way he did not look like someone to tangle with. Their driver made sure they were all inside the room before he left.

Cindy chose her seat, facing the door. From that seat she could also keep an eye on the man in the corner. She settled in as though she owned the place, and it must have had an affect because all eyes were on her. Dimitri would have been proud.

In front of each player were stacks of chips. "I don't believe I've ever encountered one of these before," she said, lifting up one of the white chips.

"White is one thousand. Red is five thousand. Blue is ten thousand. Green is twenty-five thousand," the man in the corner said.

"Oh gentlemen there must be some mistake. I didn't ask to sit at the kiddy table," she said.

And in her mind a phrase her grandfather had always used when playing cards with her was running over and over. *Go big or go home.*

One of the strangers at the table glanced at the man in the corner.

So, he works for the casino and he's not just another player, she thought to herself.

"Would any players object if we bring out the black chips?" the man in the corner asked.

Levi and Jack exchanged quick glances. "Black. One hundred thousand?" Levi asked, sounding strained.

The man nodded.

Levi and Jack exchanged another quick glance.

"I'm not making you uncomfortable, am I?" Cindy asked roguishly.

"No. Bring out the black chips," Jack said.

The man disappeared and returned a couple of minutes later. He set five black chips in front of each player, bringing the total of chips in front of each person to one million by her estimation.

Look at me now, granddad.

"House rules. There will be ante before each hand played. Dealer's choice for the game."

There was a brand new deck of cards still sealed in plastic in the middle of the table.

"Who goes first?" Levi asked, sounding nervous.

Cindy made a tsk-ing sound. "Oh you poor boy. Did no one ever explain things to you? Ladies always go first."

She leaned forward, picked up the deck of cards, and peeled the plastic off it. The man in the corner quickly took it off the table where she dropped it. She sorted through the deck, tossed the two jokers to the side along with the box, and then began to shuffle.

On the third time through she was able to make the cards form a bridge despite how stiff they were. She let Jack cut the deck and then she picked it back up.

"Ante up, gentlemen," she said, tossing in a red chip.

All the men did the same.

"You know what I love?" she asked, letting her voice purr over the words. "A good game of stud."

Jeremiah was nearly out of his mind by the time he sat down on the couch in Dr. Carpenter's office. Cindy was beyond his help. All he could do was wait for the signal from her wristwatch that it was time for the police to close the net and pray that she would be safe.

"This is unexpected," Dr. Carpenter said as he looked up from the papers on his desk.

"Is it?" Jeremiah asked, in no mood to play games with the man.

"Not really, no." Dr. Carpenter took off his reading glasses and tossed them on the desk. "They took her, didn't they?"

"Yes."

"Then they are even bigger fools than I took them for."

Jeremiah just continued to stare at him.

"What I told both of you was the truth. You have the potential to have a great relationship, but you both need to overcome a few things first. Honestly, you're at a crossroad. The time has come to choose. Choose even a moment too late, though, and you will have lost her forever."

"Thanks for the advice."

"So, what now?"

"Now you're going to tell me everything."

"I don't know everything. I am paid to give them names. The names of the resort clientele that are most likely to have risk taking or addictive personalities. At first I thought they were trying to identify candidates for their gambling addiction retreats, a way to market more aggressively to those who might need it."

"But it didn't take you very long to figure out that wasn't what they were doing with the names you gave them?"

"Yes. They paid too well. Ten dollars a name is nothing. I agree, look the other way. Maybe even a hundred same thing. But a thousand dollars a name? That's too much to pay for a marketing lead for this particular business. For a moment I thought maybe they were selling the name to competitors, but I soon realized that is not it either."

"What happened?"

"They started giving me lists of people to focus on. Lists with only the wealthiest clients on them."

"Why'd you do it? You're a smart guy, very perceptive. You could do quite well somewhere else."

The man shook his head. "Ah, yes, but somewhere else they'd look a little more closely at my papers, make a few more inquiries, maybe even a phone call."

"And they'd figure out you lost your license some time ago," Jeremiah guessed.

"It is as you say."

"For what?"

"It doesn't matter. What matters is that I am good at what I do. Here I could help people. And I have. But I also know nothing lasts forever. So, I take the extra money, save it for when I have to leave."

"Tell me about Malcolm Griffith."

Dr. Carpenter frowned. "Malcolm Griffith. I saw him when he was here a week or two ago. I never put his name on the list."

Jeremiah leaned forward. "Now would not be the time to lie to me," he said, and he went ahead and let the mask slip a little, let the doctor see just how far the darkness ran through him.

The other man sucked in his breath. "I knew you weren't a nice guy."

"No, I'm not, but I am the good guy. Tell me about Malcolm."

"Malcolm was rich, yes, and he was a bit of a risk taker, as most rich men are. That's how many of them achieve the level of success they do. But he is no gambler. He has no addiction complex. And he has a very strong sense of right and wrong."

"Had," Jeremiah corrected him.

The psychologist frowned. "What do you mean?"

"I mean your friends pulled him into their little poker game. He realized it was fixed, he confronted them, and they killed him."

Dr. Carpenter's eyes widened in genuine surprise. "This isn't true."

"It is true."

"Why would they pick him? I never put him on the list."

"Greed? Just a guess. After all, you didn't put Cindy on the list either and yet she's at the game right now."

"I never thought anyone would get hurt," he said, looking genuinely contrite. "I'll help all I can, tell you all I know."

"Is Arnold one of them?" Jeremiah asked.

"No."

"How do you know, you said you didn't know everyone in their little group."

"I know he is not. He does not have the personality for it. He is a good man. And I know that they worked hard to avoid being detected by him. I figured detection one day was inevitable."

"Hence, saving up your little bribes for the day you got fired."

He nodded.

"Okay, show me everything you have."

They were nearly an hour into the game and Jack was nearly out of chips. Levi was doing only slightly better while Cindy was holding her own against the other two men. Then again, she had an advantage. She knew they were cheating and she was playing accordingly. Both Levi and Jack were still under the delusion that this was a game of skill and luck.

She just wished she knew when her moment would come. She could tell they were cheating. They were signaling to each other. It was subtle, but it was happening. So if either of them were dealing she knew to keep her bets light. She was also working to lay down a set of false tells so that she controlled what kind of hand they thought she had. It was a trick she had learned playing with her father and grandfather.

Her seven-year-old self had learned to frown at bad hands all throughout a game and to try to bluff her way through them until she got a really spectacular hand and then she would frown just as hard and raise aggressively. And they would think that once again she had nothing and she would keep raising until they called and she'd clean them out. It was a lot more sophisticated than what her seven-year-old self was capable of, but she was working the same principles here.

Jack slammed his cards down as he got taken for the rest of what he had. He was red in the face, angry. He wanted a chance to win it back. "Get me some more chips," he said.

"I'm sorry, but you've maxed your credit limit," the man in the corner said.

Jack sat there for a moment, fuming.

"Don't be a sore loser, Jack," she said, not trying to mock him, but rather trying to calm him down so he'd get out of there before he did something truly stupid.

"I am no loser," he said. He turned toward the man in the corner. "This should buy me more chips," he said. He pulled Dorothea's pearl necklace out of his jacket pocket and tossed it at the man.

Cindy barely restrained herself at the sight of it.

The man glanced at the one player at the table who nodded almost imperceptibly.

"Let me see what I can do," the man said, exiting with the necklace. He returned shortly with more chips.

It didn't matter. Within three more hands both Levi and Jack were out. They stood up and the man moved to block the door. "No one leaves until the game is done."

"This is a load of crap," Levi fumed.

And suddenly it was as though she could see what was about to play out. She could feel the anger of the two men. Jack was angry, but at this point knew to keep his mouth shut. He had, after all, used a stolen necklace as a buy-in. Levi, though, was starting to get noisy. He was on the verge of saying that there had been cheating going on, and if he didn't back down from that statement fast he was going to get himself killed.

Maybe get all of them killed. She thought about pushing the panic button. The truth was, though, as far as the cheating went it was her word against the others in the room.

She took a deep breath, picked up a couple of her black chips and threw them at Jack and Levi.

"Why don't you boys shut up and let a lady play," she said. "Or you could cause a fuss and end up with *nothing*," she said, giving her voice a slight edge to it as she'd heard Jeremiah do before when trying to intimidate someone.

And, for a miracle, it actually seemed to work.

"Alright. Now let's stop fussin' and start playing," she said.

They went four more hands and then she was dealing. She'd called five card draw this time. She ended up with the Ace, King, and Jack of hearts along with the eight of hearts and a six of spades. She stared for a moment. Her natural instinct was to get rid of the six and hope for another heart to give her a flush. She had three to the big one, though. The royal flush. Her father would tell her to play it safe, but her grandfather's words kept echoing in her head.

She tossed the six and the eight. She pulled two cards and when she saw the Queen and Ten of hearts show up as if by magic it took everything she had not to give away her excitement. She played her fake tell, letting off that she was disappointed but determined to try and recoup her losses by bluffing.

She sized up the stacks of chips in front of the other two players. When the betting came around to her she raised by one million dollars. It was not the first time she'd made that large a bet, but three of the four times she'd bet that large before she'd been bluffing and had made sure she was caught in the bluff.

Now the other two guys were sizing up her stack of chips. It was the end, it was as though they all sensed it. The guy to her left stared her dead in the eyes and then raised again. As did the guy next to him.

She licked her lips and then slid her entire pile into the center. "I'm all in, gentlemen," she said.

And after only a moment's hesitation they both did the same. "We call, little lady," the one said.

She brushed her watch with her pinky finger, pushing the button, as she flipped her cards up and over to drop them on top of the pile of chips.

"Royal flush."

Jack and Levi jumped out of their seats. Cindy braced herself for the fallout.

"That's more than five million," the man directly across from her said.

"So it is," she answered.

He glanced at the man in the corner. Her heart hammered in fear because she felt what was coming next. And when he pulled a gun out of his coat she saw it long before Jack or Levi did.

"Okay, now here's the deal-" he began.

The door flew open and he turned in surprise. Mark leaped forward, knocking the gun out of his hand and then hit him in the jaw. Two other men surged into the room behind Mark and descended on the two gamblers.

"Make sure you arrest Jack for the theft of Dorothea's pearl necklace," Cindy said as she stood up.

She was amazed that her legs would even support her weight given how shaky she felt.

"Mark, a million of this belongs to Joseph," she said.

He nodded even as he was putting the handcuffs on the gunman. Jack made a break for the door. Cindy yanked off one of her high heeled shoes and threw it at the back of his head. The heel hit him right in the back of the neck and he dropped like a stone.

"Whoa!" Levi shouted in shock.

"You think that's something, you should see what she can do with a dart," Mark said.

Seven hours later Cindy and Jeremiah were in the back of Mark's car and finally heading home. The two women, the masseuse, a janitor, and Dr. Carpenter had all been arrested along with the three men from the casino.

It turned out that the masseuse, Lancaster, had been the brains of the group. He had successfully run similar schemes at two other resorts around the country. Once on the inside he had manipulated the old yoga teacher into leaving so Summer could take her place.

Malcolm had been killed at the poker game when he surmised the game was rigged. He had been killed by the same man who would have shot Jack, Levi, and Cindy. Lancaster and the janitor had buried the body.

As soon as the handcuffs had gone on the front desk woman had rolled over on the others, telling the police everything she knew, including the location of the grave.

When Cindy and Jeremiah had finally left, Arnold had extended an open invitation to return any time for free.

Cindy was exhausted as she finished telling Mark and Jeremiah just how the poker game had gone.

"You should have seen her throw her shoe, though. That was the best part," Mark said.

"Dorothea got her necklace back, I'm glad," Cindy said.

"Yeah. Apparently Jack has a history of stealing baubles for his wife. She's going down for it, too, as an accessory."

"What about Kim and Levi?" Cindy asked.

"Idiots, greedy idiots, but they were clean."

"I can't believe it's already Friday," Jeremiah said.

"I haven't gone to bed yet, it's still Thursday, I don't care what the clock says," Mark protested.

"I'm going to sleep all day tomorrow, or today, or whatever," Cindy vowed.

"I think we all will," Mark said grimly.

They made it to Cindy's house first just as dawn was touching the sky. Jeremiah carried her bag up to the door for her. "Meet you Saturday morning for Valentine's breakfast?" he asked.

"That sounds good."

He leaned in, gave her a quick kiss, and then was headed back to the car.

"Valentine's Day," she whispered, and then smiled. It had been a long time coming.

22

It was Saturday morning and Cindy had just parked in the parking lot of the restaurant where she was meeting Jeremiah for breakfast. He had just beat her there and was standing right outside his car. She got out of her car, walked over and hugged Jeremiah tight. "I missed you last night," she admitted.

"I missed you, too. Happy Valentine's Day."

"Happy Valentine's Day," she said with a grin. She stepped back and reached down and grabbed his hand. She gave it a squeeze and he squeezed back. Hand-in-hand they walked to the door.

"I'm starving," she admitted as her stomach growled noisily.

"Yeah, I could eat-"

Jeremiah dropped her hand as he stopped talking. Startled she glanced at him. He was staring at something behind her.

"What's wrong?" she asked.

Before he could answer her she heard someone behind her call out, "Morning, Cindy, Rabbi."

She turned and saw that Gus and a couple of the church members involved in the drama ministry were walking toward them.

"Good morning," she said, struggling to regain her composure.

"Morning," Jeremiah said, his voice sounding a little distant.

The three men walked inside and as soon as the door had closed behind them Cindy turned to Jeremiah.

"You stopped holding my hand because you saw them," she accused.

"Yes."

"That wasn't cool."

"We talked about this."

"You talked about this. I've heard all your reasons that we should keep our whatever this is a secret. We can't do that forever, though. Frankly, I don't want to keep it a secret anymore."

"I'm not ready to put us through that."

She took a deep breath. Anger was rushing through her. Having him drop her hand that way had upset her and then embarrassed her. The truth was that Gus and the others had probably seen them holding hands anyway which made him dropping her hand that much more humiliating.

"You say you're not ashamed to be seen with me, but you are scared," she said.

"Yes, and you should be, too."

"Well, I'm not. And you know what? I'll put your mind at ease. You don't have to stress out about dinner tonight and where we're going or who will be seeing us or what we can and can't do. Dinner is off."

"Cindy, don't do that."

"Then promise me that you'll hold my hand on the table regardless of who is in the restaurant."

He stared at her, but didn't say anything.

"That's what I thought," she said, turning and heading toward her car.

"What about breakfast?" he called after her.

"Not hungry!"

She got in her car, slammed the door shut and moments later was speeding out of the parking lot. She noticed he was still standing in front of the restaurant watching her go.

She hadn't made it more than half a block down the road before the tears hit.

Jeremiah's frustration was slowly giving way to fear. It had been five hours since Cindy had left him standing in front of the restaurant, and she still wasn't answering her phone. He had even tried going over to her house, but she wasn't home.

Finally, he got out his phone and called Geanie.

"Hello, Jeremiah?" she asked, sounding surprised when she answered the phone.

"Yes, I need to know where Cindy's going to be tonight."

"Um, I thought she was going to be at dinner with you. Is that no longer the case?"

"Yes, we had...a fight this morning."

"Were you an idiot?" Geanie asked bluntly.

"Excuse me?"

"Cindy is crazy in love with you and she avoids conflict and confrontation in relationships like the plague. Plus she was really excited about being able to go out with you tonight. Therefore, in order for the two of you to have actually had a fight I surmise that you had to do something pretty epically stupid."

"I refused to hold her hand this morning when people we knew were around. She was pretty angry. She's not answering my calls, and I need to apologize."

There was a sigh on the other end of the phone. "Okay, let me call her and find out where she's going to be tonight."

"Okay."

He ended the call then waited. Five minutes later Geanie called back and he answered immediately.

"Well, the good news is I know where she's going to be. The bad news for you is that it's a very public place."

"Where is she going to be?"

"She's going to be volunteering at the Valentine's dinner at the church tonight. There'll be a lot of people from First Shepherd there. I believe there's even some families from the synagogue who are going."

"Okay."

"Are you going to actually go?" Geanie asked.

"I think I have to. If I don't try to make this right tonight then tomorrow might be too late."

"So, you're going to apologize to her?"

"Yes."

"Have you gotten her a present yet?"

"No, I haven't had time to do anything like that."

"Get her red roses. It's sort of the universal symbol of the holiday, plus most of us are a sucker for them."

"Okay, thanks for the advice. Are you and Joseph going to the dinner?"

"No, we're going camping. Going to a church function like that as a staff member, even if you're not supposed to be working you end up working."

"I understand. Well, I hope you have a wonderful evening."

"Thanks, you, too. You know, Cindy's never had a real boyfriend before. And unfortunately, even though you reciprocate her feelings, in many ways she still doesn't have one. You understand?"

"Yes," he said, trying to get his emotions under control.

"Secret romances can be fun for a little while, but they pale in comparison to the thrill of pointing to the object of your affection and saying 'that's my guy'.

"And I'm robbing her of that."

"Yes."

"I know. Thanks for the help. I need to get to the store."

"You're welcome. Good luck."

Jeremiah ended the call, grabbed his keys, and headed outside. He'd had nearly half a year to figure out how to best let people know that they were dating without creating more headaches than either of them were willing to deal with. He hadn't come up with anything. Not that he'd tried overly hard.

To be honest, he had still expected Cindy to wake up one day, come to her senses, and decide she didn't want to be with him after all. It was possible she might still do that, but to lose her because he wasn't willing to be open about their relationship was unacceptable. G-d had brought them this far. It was up to Jeremiah to make the next move.

Cindy was miserable. She felt like she was walking around the gymnasium in a fog. It was Valentine's Day and she was wearing her new red dress. Instead of being out at a nice dinner, though, she was stuck here serving dinner to a lot of happy couples and families. It had been her first chance in her life to have a proper Valentine's Day date, and she was upset that it had fallen apart. She had told herself that coming down and volunteering at the church event would be better than sitting home alone wallowing in her sadness and frustration. She was beginning to think that maybe she had been wrong about that.

She kept telling herself that it was stupid. February 14th was just a day like any other. And in the grand scheme of things she really was far more upset with the fact that Jeremiah was having such a hard time being public about them dating or quasi-dating or whatever it was that they were doing. Was it too much to ask that they be able to hold hands in public and that she be able to tell people he was her boyfriend?

She understood everything that he'd said. She knew that it wasn't as simple for them as it was for most couples. She was tired of having to keep it secret, though. And, realistically, if they couldn't tell anyone, what future could they really ever hope to have together?

One thing was for sure, the way things were now was slowly killing her. Sometimes she felt that he really did want her to release him from their relationship, whatever it was. What if she did, though? She could never go back to being just friends with him, not after everything that had happened. And the thought of not having him in her life was too much for her to take.

"Cindy, you okay?"

She turned and saw Dave staring at her, a worried expression on his face.

"I'm fine," she said, although she could barely manage a smile.

"For what it's worth, I'm sorry to see you here tonight. You look wonderful, though."

"Thanks. I'm surprised you're here."

He shrugged. "Long story. I'm glad to see you're at least wearing the dress."

She took a deep breath. "It's my party dress, and it's a party. I kind of had to wear it."

Dave gave her a sad smile, and then his eyes drifted past her. "Well, I think I know at least one person who will appreciate it."

She turned to look in the direction he was staring and her heart skipped a beat. Jeremiah was standing just inside the door, scanning the crowd. He was wearing a dark suit and holding a bouquet of red roses. He spotted her and strode toward her quickly, a determined look on his face. He passed right by Mark, Traci, and the babies seemingly without even noticing them. A family from his synagogue waved and he didn't so much as glance in their direction.

At last Jeremiah stopped in front of her and handed her the roses. "These are for you," he said.

"Thank you, they're beautiful," she said as she took them from him.

"I am truly, deeply sorry. You are the best thing that has ever happened to me, and you will never be able to understand just how much you mean to me. I'm sorry that I've allowed my fear to hurt you, to get in the way of us being able to have a real relationship."

She could feel tears beginning to form as she struggled to get words out. "It's okay. I understand. Everything you said makes sense."

"Is it too late for me to hold your hand in public?" he asked, eyes boring intently into hers as though they were piercing her very soul. Slowly he held out his right hand to her.

She stared at it for a moment, heart racing. He was offering a public display of affection, the kind he had refused earlier that had led to the fight. She knew what a big deal it was, what it had probably cost him.

"No, it's not too late to hold my hand," she said, her voice cracking slightly with emotion. She extended her left hand, and touched his. They were palm to palm for a moment. Then he closed his fingers around her hand.

He closed his eyes for just a moment, and she would have given anything to know what he was thinking right then. When he opened his eyes again there was something shining in them, a light that was fierce and soft all at the same time.

And then suddenly, still holding her hand, he sank down on one knee. Gasps went up all around the room and everything grew completely silent as Cindy stared at him, wondering what he was doing.

"Cindy Preston, when we met nearly three years ago I was an empty husk of a man, living the life of a ghost. And then, I heard you scream, and I came to your rescue, or so I thought. I had no idea then that you were actually the one rescuing me. Every time I tried to stay away from you, telling myself it was better, God kept leading me straight back to you. I was falling and there was nothing I could do about it. I have never been so helpless in my entire life.

"But I was afraid. Afraid of the challenges, afraid of letting you in and letting you see the real me. And one by one you crushed those fears. You lifted me up and made me a better man. You have seen me at my worst. And now all I want is to spend a lifetime working to make sure you see me at my best."

He reached into his jacket with his free hand and pulled out a small box. He flipped open the lid and she stared in shock at a golden ring with a heart-shaped diamond.

"Cindy Preston, I'm asking you in the sight of God and all these witnesses if you will grant me the privilege of standing by your side and protecting you and loving you always. Will you do me the honor of consenting to be my wife?"

Jeremiah's eyes were shining, but it was hard to see them through her own tears. She nodded her head mutely until she finally found her voice.

"Yes, Jeremiah, I will marry you," she said.

He took the ring from the box and slid it onto her finger. Then he stood up and the room erupted in cheers and applause and more noise than she'd ever heard in her life, but it all fell away as he took her in his arms and kissed her.

His lips were soft and warm against hers, and she could feel his arms around her, supporting her. She didn't know how long they were like that, but it seemed that the kiss would last an entire lifetime.

Then she felt more arms coming around her and she looked up and saw Mark and Traci's faces. They were both crying and hugging her and Jeremiah in one big, group hug. Dave rushed forward and was clapping Jeremiah on the back.

Jeremiah finally let go of her, and she turned and hugged Traci tightly as they both kept crying. When she let go she turned to see Geanie and Joseph standing there, beaming.

"We made it just in time!" Geanie said.

"You knew?" Cindy asked bewildered, as she reached out to hug her as well.

"We had a feeling," Joseph said right before Jeremiah wrapped him in a bear hug. "We were almost at the campsite when Jeremiah called us. We turned around and drove as fast as we could because we didn't want to miss this."

Cindy felt dizzy and out of breath. She couldn't believe what was happening. After she hugged Joseph both Traci and Geanie grabbed her hand to admire her ring and Cindy found herself staring at it in awe.

"I've never seen a heart shaped diamond before!" Traci squealed.

It was breathtaking. And it was hers. Just as Jeremiah was hers. She turned back to look at him and was stunned to see that his cheeks were wet with tears as well. She gave him a quick kiss, reveling in the fact that she could do that in public. Now all the world would know what they meant to each other.

"I have a fiancé," she said.

"And soon you'll have a husband, for real," he said softly.

Look for

BROTHERHOOD OF LIES

a Tex Ravencroft Adventure

Coming Soon!

Debbie Viguié is the New York Times Bestselling author of more than three dozen novels including the *Wicked* series, the *Crusade* series and the *Wolf Springs Chronicles* series co-authored with Nancy Holder. Debbie also writes thrillers including *The Psalm 23 Mysteries,* the *Kiss* trilogy, and the *Witch Hunt* trilogy. When Debbie isn't busy writing she enjoys spending time with her husband, Scott, visiting theme parks. They live in Florida with their cat, Schrödinger.

Made in the USA
Lexington, KY
24 July 2015